DANICA FLYNN

The CHASE

THE CHASE

A PHILADELPHIA BULLDOGS BOOK

DANICA FLYNN

The Chase

Copyright © 2022 Danica Flynn
This is a work of fiction. Names, characters, businesses, places, events, and incidents are either products of the author's imagination or used in a fictitious manner. Any resemblance to actual persons, living or dead, or actual events is purely coincidental.
All rights reserved.

ebook ISBN: 978-1-957494-00-5
Print ISBN: 978-1-957494-01-2

Cover Photography: ArtOfPhotos/ Shutterstock
Cover Design: Emily's World Of Design
Editor: Charlie Knight

Content Note: This book deals with mental illness such as anxiety and night terrors. There are panic attacks on page.

To TK and Hayes for being my personality inspirations for TJ.

PLAYLIST

"Eye of the Tiger" by Survivor
"I Knew You Were Trouble" By Taylor Swift
"Boyfriend" by Tegan and Sara
"We fell in love in October" by Girl in Red
"Boyfriend" By Best Coast
"Party in the U.S.A." By Miley Cyrus
"Going Gets Tough" By The Growlers
"Call me Maybe" By Carly Rae Jepsen
"Silver Lining" By Mt.Joy
"Soft" By Babygirl
"Are You Gonna Be My Girl" By Jet
"Sleep All Day" By The Rural Alberta Advantage
"Friday I'm in Love" By The Cure
"You're Somebody Else" By Flora Cash
"When I'm With You" By Best Coast

CHAPTER ONE

TJ
OCTOBER

I grinned at my buddy Noah as I climbed on top of the barstool. He gave me a warning look and mouthed 'don't,' but where Noah was all quiet seriousness, I was loud and obnoxious. Noah's tiny girlfriend, Dinah, sidled up beside him. She gave me a wink as she pulled him down into a passionate kiss to distract him.

Atta girl, D!

"BOYS!" I shouted into the packed sports bar full of equal parts hockey players and fans. Naturally, all eyes were on me. Not gonna lie, I liked being the center of attention. "Let's get fucking LIT!"

My teammates erupted into cheers like the hooligans they were and egged me on. G, our captain, shook his head, and I saw Riley nod while he snuck out the door. Since Riley got married, he hadn't been much for going out. He used to be my bud with banging bunnies, but married life made him boring.

"Hey, asshole, get off my barstool!" the bartender with the shaved head yelled at me.

The owner, a big, blonde middle-aged guy, stood next to his son while he shook his head with a laugh. Hal Holmstrom didn't mind the team coming in and causing chaos, partly because he was an ex-Bulldog. I liked to think he encouraged my antics.

I gave them my signature Desjardins lopsided grin and a shrug as if to say, 'Who me?'

"You know I'm good for business, Ayden!" I teased the surly one of the two.

Ayden threw me a death glare. "Get down!"

Noah tugged on the hem of my slacks to get me off the stool.

I jumped down and eyed the redheaded rookie defenseman, Logan Cullen. "Come on Cully—you're buying!"

"One round. I got a kid to get home to," Logan said, but he saddled up to the bar and bought a round for the team, anyway.

Noah shook his head at me and wrapped his arms around his girl. Dinah looked up at him with stars in her eyes while he kissed her temple. They were so sickeningly in love, but I was happy for my friends. Especially since I spent years watching Noah pine over our neighbor.

Logan handed me and Noah a beer each before he delivered beers to the rest of the team. He was a good sport, but it didn't mean we would go easy on him. Rookies knew we had to bust their balls at all times. It was hockey law.

"You're so extra, T," Dinah laughed.

I grinned at her and loosened my tie. I loved being a hockey player but having to wear suits to games was annoying as hell. I couldn't wait to get out of this monkey suit...and preferably with a woman crawling naked into my bed.

I didn't want to admit it, but since I got back from playing in the World Hockey Championship last summer, I'd had a bit of a dry spell. Not that there weren't bunnies already eyeing me up and offering, but lately, they'd lost their appeal.

"Home opener, baby!" I cheered.

Dinah kicked my foot. "You still have eighty more games to play. I've suffered through watching this team my entire life; I know not to be hopeful."

"Lovey!" Noah groaned.

She gave me a wicked smile.

Dinah did not mince words about how she felt about our team. She was a hardcore hockey fan, but like a lot of Philly fans, it came with some hopelessness. I didn't blame her, especially because last season sucked. That's why I was amped about winning the home opener. It was a fresh new season, and I was ready to bring the cup back to this city.

"We're gonna prove you wrong!" I said and took a sip of my beer.

"Bring me the cup!"

Noah and I shared an amused look. "Damn, Kens, your girl's a ball buster, eh?"

He grinned and kissed her neck. "Yeah. I guess I'll keep her, though."

Dinah laughed. "I'm like the worst WAG ever! But sorry, bud, I love hockey."

I rolled my eyes. "We know!"

I scanned the bar, looking for my twin sister. We usually hashed out the games together. As much as Noah was my best bud on the ice, Roxie was my literal best friend. Her opinion about my game always meant a lot to me. Like

Dinah, she didn't mince words. My sister was kind of an asshole, but that's what I loved about her.

I spied her at the end of the bar, where Benny had his arms wrapped around her. I couldn't say I was happy about Roxie getting with my teammate, the big guy broke the code, but I've never seen her happier. I watched them fight for three years straight over some bullshit thing he said when he first met her, so it wasn't a surprise when they finally got together. I only wished I didn't find out by coming home and hearing them have sex. The thought of it still made me want to puke.

I watched Roxie sip on her beer while she talked animatedly to a petite blonde. A blonde with a nice ass. The mystery blonde turned for a second, giving me a glimpse of her profile, and my breath caught in my throat when I realized who it was.

Noah nudged me. "Dude, is that Maxine?"

"Who's Maxine?" Dinah asked.

"Nobody," I muttered.

Noah raised an eyebrow at me with a knowing look.

Last summer, I asked Maxine for her number, and then like the chicken I was, never asked her out.

"Max works in sales for the team," Noah said.

"What did you do?" Dinah asked and pinned me with a death glare. Dinah might have been a tiny little thing, but she could be intense.

"Nothing," I said with a shrug and sipped on my beer, hoping they would drop the conversation already.

"The same thing he always does," Noah said.

I cut a glare at him.

"Oh, T, what did you do?" Dinah asked.

"Nothing."

"He asked for her number and then never called her," Noah said.

Dinah moved out of Noah's arms and punched me in the arm. The petite woman could hit pretty hard. "Ow! You hit like a hockey player. You're worse than Roxie."

She grinned. "I have three meathead older brothers. Who do you think taught me?"

"But what was that for?" I whined and rubbed my arm.

She put her hands on her hips and arched an eyebrow at me. "Why are you the way you are?"

I gave her my lopsided grin. "I don't want to be tied down!"

Lie.

Huge lie.

Despite being known as the guy on the team who only hit it and quit it, lately it hadn't appealed to me. I was getting older; that might explain why sowing my wild oats was getting stale.

I glanced around the bar and noticed three different women eyeing me up. I could walk up to all three of them and ask them if they wanted to suck my dick in the bathroom, and they would do it, no questions asked. Not that I would. I wasn't *that* big of an asshole. But it felt like they never saw me for *me*. I didn't realize that bothered me until I messed up things with Taylor.

Last year, I found an awesome girl, and I let her slip through my fingers. It had been nice having someone care about me. Someone who saw me as TJ and not just TJ Desjardins, star hockey player for the Philadelphia Bulldogs. I fucked up with Taylor, big time. Instead of dealing with it then, I went to Russia for the World Hockey Championships. When I got back and finally called her, she had already moved on.

I was good for a quick lay, but women didn't see me as long-term. I used to be okay with that; I used to want that. But now I wasn't so sure.

"You're the literal worst!" Dinah sighed.

Noah wrapped his arms around her and whispered something in her ear that I couldn't hear. She nodded and pursed her lips.

"T, we want you to be happy," Dinah said.

I gave her a big smile. "I'm happy. We won!"

She shook her head and laughed. "Okay, bud. Now win some more."

I was only half-paying attention to Dinah because I'd locked eyes with the blonde woman talking to my sister. She gave me a small smile in recognition and turned back around.

The reason I never called Maxine? She was too good for me. Maxine had 'good girl' written all over her. I flirted with her, and she laughed at my jokes, but she was wife material, and I wasn't sure I deserved someone like her.

That didn't mean my horny brain had lost interest, though.

Seeing Maxine in that slinky black dress and thigh-high boots made my dick kick against my zipper. Those boots looked like the kind I could easily imagine wrapped around my back while I pounded into her and she moaned my name.

"Bro, don't do it," Noah warned.

"Do what?" I asked innocently.

I waggled my eyebrows at him and then crossed to the bar where the pretty blonde was downing her glass of wine. Sometimes I couldn't help myself.

CHAPTER TWO

MAXINE

"What happened?" my boss and new friend Rox cried.

I held up one manicured finger while I downed my entire glass of wine.

Rox cackled at that and leaned back against the broad chest of her massive hockey player boyfriend. Benny gave me a sympathetic smile. They were both gigantic hockey players compared to my five-foot-five frame, but they were so cute together. They were the hottest couple I'd ever seen. Benny had dark brown skin and huge muscles, while Rox was this gorgeous curvy woman with a Snow White complexion and perfect make-up. Sometimes I was jealous of how put together and glamorous she looked all the time.

"He didn't show up," I said as I set my empty glass on the bar.

I rubbed my temples in frustration. I hadn't properly dated since high school and that had ended in blood and tears. Literally. After the car accident that killed my boyfriend and my parents, I gave up on love.

Instead, I had the occasional hookup that always made me feel bad about myself afterwards. People talked about sex being freeing, but it always made me feel guilty. I'd blame that on my strict religious upbringing; my parents had drilled it into my head that sex was only for marriage and procreation. Needless to say, I had some complicated feelings about sex.

The only reason I agreed to the date tonight was because my bestie, Keiana, knew the guy from nursing school. I would have understood if he got called into work, but ghosting me and not showing up told me who he was. Just another jerk who didn't have time for me. I couldn't say it was the first time it had happened, either.

"Oh, Max, I'm so sorry," Rox offered.

Benny narrowed his dark eyes. "Do I need to do something to this guy?"

I shook my head. "Nah, but I appreciate your support."

Rox glared at her boyfriend. "No fighting."

"Whatever you say, angel." He kissed her temple.

I sighed and was about to ask the bartender for another drink when I felt a presence sidle up behind me.

"Can I buy you a drink?" a deep voice asked from behind me.

A familiar one.

I turned and came face-to-face with TJ Desjardins, hot hockey player and Rox's twin brother. His hazel eyes bored into me, and I had to remind myself that he was trouble with a capital T.

Last summer, TJ asked for my number, but when he never called, I shrugged it off. Rox warned me her brother wasn't boyfriend material, so I thought nothing of it. He made it pretty clear I wasn't the girl for him. He was a notorious playboy, and falling into bed with him wasn't a good idea. It didn't matter how hot he was.

"Tristan," Rox said in a warning tone.

It was always weird to me that Rox was the only person who called TJ by his full name. I hadn't been sure where 'TJ' came from, but Rox told me that when their mom got tired of yelling 'Tristan James' whenever he was in trouble, it got shortened to 'TJ.' Rox and their parents still called him Tristan, but to everyone else, he was TJ.

I waved her off. "Hey, TJ. Good game tonight."

"Aw, thanks, baby girl," TJ said with his signature lopsided grin.

I rolled my eyes at him. TJ was the definition of the playboy hockey player, so this 'baby girl' nonsense was not a shocker.

"Tristan," Rox snapped.

I watched Benny slide her dark hair off her shoulder and kiss her neck. I think he did it to distract her, because she closed her eyes and bit her blood-red lips at whatever he whispered in her ear. I could guarantee it was something really dirty by the way she turned around and looked up at him like he hung the moon for her.

"What are you drinking?" TJ asked me.

"Pinot Grigio, please."

His hazel eyes darkened at the word 'please,' and then he smiled. "You got it."

"Another, Max?" Ayden, the bartender, asked as he took my empty glass.

I went to high school with Ayden and the rest of the Holmstrom clan. They were a bunch of big blonde hockey players, his little sister included. Ayden's dad used to play for the Bulldogs back in the day, but when he retired, he and his teammate opened this bar in South Philly near the arena.

I think they did all right business-wise, especially when TJ brought in crowds with little stunts like the one he pulled tonight. It certainly got the attention of the puck bunnies who hung around. Like the five who were glaring at me because TJ's hand was on my back.

I pointed to TJ. "He's buying," I said to Ayden.

The two men exchanged money, and I rolled my eyes at the way they sized each other up.

Men.

TJ placed the glass of wine in my hand, and I took it with thanks. I noticed Rox and Benny were nowhere in sight, but I had a good idea what they were up to.

I was pretty sure Benny distracted his girlfriend with sex so his teammate could hit on me.

"You look nice," TJ said.

His eyes burned across my body, like he was mentally peeling the dress off of me. A part of me wondered what it would be like if he did.

"Oh...I was supposed to have a date."

He furrowed his brow and took a swig of his beer. "Supposed to?"

I shrugged. "Same old story. The guy never calls, he ghosts me, or doesn't show up at all."

TJ cringed and ran a hand through his short-cropped dark hair. "Listen, Max—"

I held up my hand. "It's fine. I'm used to it."

He gave me a look of pity, which boiled my blood. I was sick of pity. I was twenty-five years old and had endured enough pity when I became an orphan at eighteen. I was used to people feeling sorry for 'that poor girl.' I already felt so guilty for surviving when they didn't, and the pity from others didn't help.

I sipped on my wine, and TJ ran a hand across his five o'clock shadow. Not for the first time, I noticed he had big hands, and I wondered what else was big.

Okay, I was supremely horny.

"It's okay, TJ. I know what you're about," I said, breaking the silence between us.

Everyone knew. Rox had alluded to him being hurt in high school, but she refused to explain. It wasn't my business, so I didn't pry. The TJ who flirted with me last summer and asked for my number was cocky and a real charmer, but the one standing in front of me looked nervous. The difference confused me.

He gave me that lopsided grin again, and it made his eyes sparkle. He reached up and tucked a strand of my hair behind my ear. I knew that was a move. He looked like he wanted to devour me while his hand lingered on my face. I didn't mind the hungry look in his eyes, though. I kinda liked it and wanted him to keep on touching me.

"I have to say..." he started.

I sipped on my wine. "What's that?"

His finger traced down my cheek, making its slow, tortuous way down my body until he fingered the strap on my dress. He smirked, and I felt it go all the way down to my core. He leaned over and whispered in my ear, "I think this would look way better on my floor."

I should have been shocked, but since this was TJ, I wasn't. Rox had clued me in on how he liked to 'hit it and quit it' and assured me that I was better off without my heart broken. That was the thing Rox didn't know, though; my heart had already broken, so it didn't matter. I was used to men taking what they wanted from me and tossing me aside. TJ was no different.

I cocked an eyebrow at him. "Is that a promise?"

He grinned at me. "Finish your wine."

"Okay!" I cheered and downed it in one big gulp.

I wasn't usually this brazen, but after being stood up again, I thought I deserved a little fun. With TJ, that was all it would be—just some fun to pass the time.

TJ gave me an appraising look. "Atta girl."

"You want to get out of here?"

He grinned again. "Most definitely."

CHAPTER THREE

TJ

"You want another glass of wine?" I asked Maxine as she unzipped her boots and left them at the front door.

She peered up at me through eyelashes that accented her ice-blue eyes. "That's not why I came here."

Straight to the point, I hadn't expected that from her. "Okay then!"

She gave me a shy smile as I took her hand and led her to my bedroom. I unlinked our hands while I shut the door behind us. When I turned back around, she stood near the edge of my bed, fiddling with the hem of her dress. She looked nervous, unlike the woman who had downed her full glass of wine and made it obvious what she wanted from me.

I walked over to her and tilted her chin up to look at me. "You sure about this?" I asked.

She nodded.

I gave her my cockiest grin. "You know..."

"What?"

"I still think your dress would look much better on the floor."

She bit her lip and blew out a nervous breath.

I tucked her blonde hair behind her ear and cupped her face. Yeah, that might have been my signature move, but it seemed to relax her. I took that as the green light and slanted my mouth on hers. She opened to me when I flicked my tongue against the seam of her lips, and she pressed her hands against my chest. I smiled into our kiss as I felt her undo my tie while I kissed the breath out of her.

My hands roamed down her body as we kissed, and she shivered as I grazed against her nipples. I broke the kiss to gauge if that was all right, and when she nodded, I pressed my lips against her neck. She tipped back her head and moaned while I licked and sucked at her soft flesh.

"TJ," she moaned.

I danced my hand up her thigh until I was met with the soft flesh of her mound, where I had been expecting sexy underwear. My dick kicked against my zipper at the discovery she wasn't wearing any panties. I slid my finger down, barely ghosting across her slit.

"Please," she moaned.

"What, baby girl?"

She growled out like she couldn't say the words, like she needed me to take control. I pressed a thick finger against her entrance.

"You're a naughty girl, huh?" I growled into her ear as I pressed my finger inside her.

She shook her head while she bit back a moan.

"No?" I asked and gave her my lopsided smirk.

I added a second and slid my thick fingers in and out slowly. I grazed my thumb against her clit, and she rocked against my hand. She was a greedy girl, begging with her body for me to find that spot deep inside.

"TJ," she groaned.

She whimpered when I removed my hand.

"Not wearing any panties tonight...so naughty," I purred. I brought my fingers to my lips and slid them into my mouth. "Mmm, you taste good."

A blush rose up her neck, but when she looked at me, her eyes were dark with desire. I loved when a woman looked at me like that. "Please," she begged.

Before I could say anything else, she reached behind her and unzipped her dress. The slinky material fell to the floor, revealing a sexy black bra. She unclasped that too, letting it drop to the floor on top of the heap that was her dress.

It *did* look pretty good on my floor.

"Get on the bed," I growled.

I took off my tie and shed my suit jacket. I tossed it aside and made quick work of the buttons of my dress shirt. She obliged and laid back on my bed with her blonde hair framing around the pillow, making her look angelic. My dick hurt at the sight of her naked and waiting in my bed. There was nothing more beautiful than a woman on her back with her legs spread wide for me. Nothing.

I took off the rest of my clothes in record time and crawled into bed beside her. I cupped her face and kissed her again. She moaned into my mouth and snaked her hands into my hair. I closed my eyes and lost myself in the taste of her lips on mine. We were a mess of fiery kisses and hands roaming while I rolled on top of her, pinning her beneath me. Our tongues battled a war with each other while she raked her fingers through my hair. Her touch set my body on fire, and I couldn't wait to be pressed so deep inside her, it made her scream my name.

I broke the kiss and stared down at her. Her pale face was flushed, and there was a splotch of red across her chest. Her lips were plump and bruised from our desperate kisses. I cradled her jaw in my hand and rubbed my thumb on her bottom lip. I wanted to watch those lips wrap around my dick, but I'd definitely blow my load too soon. I needed to be inside her first.

"What?" she asked.

"You're so gorgeous," I breathed out.

That wasn't a lie. I might have had a lot of women in this bed, but Maxine stood out in a crowd. From her bright blonde hair to her smoking hot body, she was a woman who demanded my attention.

"Are you gonna give me that thing or what?" she asked.

'That Thing' being my dick, which was poking into her leg aggressively.

I laughed, but I reached down to give her clit some feather-light touches. "That depends on if you're ready for me. You ready, baby?"

She ground against my hand. "I'm ready."

I gave her that lopsided grin again while I reached into the bedside table and pulled out a condom. She shifted on the bed to get comfortable while I slid the latex on. I spread her thighs and positioned myself between them. I didn't enter her at first; instead, I toyed with her clit with the head of my cock. I teased her with it, giving her a taste of what was to come.

She whimpered beneath me and arched her body up like she was trying to do the job herself.

"You want this, huh?" I asked as I circled against her clit, not giving her what she wanted quite yet.

"Please," she begged.

I loved when women begged for my dick.

I gave her a grin and slid home for the first time. I groaned when she wrapped her legs around me and pulled me in deeper. She felt *so* good. I had to be careful I didn't come too soon.

I rolled my hips against her, sliding all the way out and then back in again while I pulled one of her legs higher around my waist. She let me take the lead while the headboard banged against the wall every time I moved above her. She dug her nails into my back and moved in time with me. I wasn't sure what was louder, the creak of the bed, the headboard thwacking against the wall, or her cries of pleasure.

"Come for me, baby girl," I ordered as I peered down at her lithe body beneath me. My large bulk made her seem even smaller than she already was.

Her eyes snapped open, and those blue orbs looked up at me timidly. Max was not my typical type. She had 'good girl' written all over her, and I was fucking that good girl into oblivion. The worst part? I liked it. I liked that I convinced her to be bad with me tonight.

That probably made me an asshole, but it wasn't like she didn't know what I was about. My playboy reputation preceded me. Max knew I was in it for a good time, not a long time.

I quickened my pace, driving into her hard while she screamed out my name. Something about her cries seemed oddly rehearsed, but I wasn't thinking about that when at any second, the feeling of her pussy wrapped around my cock was going to make me come.

I leaned my head against the crook of her neck and gave her tiny kisses until my lips were on the shell of her ear. "Good girl," I purred. "You're gonna make me come."

"Okay."

She locked her heels together around my waist and dug her nails into my back while I continued to pound into her. I took her like an animal, thrusting and rutting into her hard and fast until she cried out loudly beneath me. When her cries hit a crescendo, I let go. My body tingled while I rocked inside her and came so hard I thought I saw stars.

I took a second to catch my breath, then I cupped her face once more and brought my lips down to hers for one last kiss.

I only pulled away so I could get rid of the condom. I rolled off of her and went into my bathroom.

When I came back out, she was standing up and struggling to zip up her dress. I frowned at that. I was looking forward to round two, where she wrapped those pretty lips of hers around my cock, and I came down her throat. After I sucked on her clit until she begged for it, of course. I might be an asshole, but I was an equal opportunity guy when it came to oral.

She jumped when I brushed her hair over her shoulder and pressed a kiss on her neck. "Where'd you think you're going?" I asked.

"Home?"

I moved her hands off the zipper of her dress. "I'm not done with you yet."

She grimaced. "I have work tomorrow."

I sighed. Right, I forgot about that.

I reluctantly zipped up her dress for her. "I'll give you a ride home."

"No!" she snapped while she turned around. When she saw my taken aback look, she chewed on her bottom lip. "Sorry. We've both been drinking. I'll call a car."

"I got it."

She waved me off. "It's fine, T. I'll see you around."

Before I could protest again, she was gone in a flash, and the door slammed behind her. I rubbed my hand over the back of my neck and slumped down on my bed.

Having sex always made me feel better, especially when the loneliness cut in. But watching her run out of my condo minutes after we were done fucking made that tiny, insecure voice whisper in my ear. It told me I would never be good enough. That I was just a quick fuck, so she could brag about sleeping with a hockey player. I didn't know Max that well, but I didn't think she was a puck bunny looking for a WAG title. It made me wonder if I had done something wrong.

Her cries had been a bit loud. And porny sounding. I scrubbed my hand over my face. I didn't know what I did, but something told me I fucked up.

I wasn't sure why I even cared. She was just the quick lay I needed to dust off my dry spell. It wasn't like I wanted more with her.

CHAPTER FOUR

MAXINE

"You're home late. Good date?" my bestie and roommate Keiana called out when I opened the door to the row house we shared in South Philly.

"Jiminy Cricket!" I yelled in surprise at the sound of her voice. I thought she was on shift tonight and hadn't expected her to be home. Or up at this hour.

I toed off my boots and walked into the living room, where she was sitting up watching TV. She tipped back her head, and her long box braids fell back behind the couch. "You can swear, Max!"

"You know it's hard for me! I like to save it up for a rainy day," I said as I slumped onto the couch beside her.

After my family died, Keiana was the only family I had left. I had an aunt in Michigan, but since I was an adult and had been about to move into the dorms at UPenn, I never went to live with her. She still sends me cards on my birthday, but we're not close.

When I got the internship with the Bulldogs in my last year of college, Kei let me move in with her and her new husband. Her place was close to the arena, so it was perfect. When her husband left and the team offered me the full-time position, I never moved out. It worked out because she needed help with the mortgage, and I liked living with my best friend.

I loved living in South Philly. I didn't love how much the rideshare cost me to get home, though. Maybe I should have let TJ call me one instead. Not like he couldn't afford it on his salary.

Kei's black-brown eyes stared at me from over the couch. "Was the date good?"

I grimaced at her.

"Bad? But it looks like you have whisker burn on your chest, so..." She trailed off, and a wide smile spread across her dark complexion.

"He didn't show up!" I fumed.

Her face fell. "What? What the hell! Wait, I'm confused because you look like you just got fucked."

I cringed at her words. I wasn't a total prude; it was just that my parents drilled into me that swearing wasn't 'lady-like.' It was a hard habit to break when you were told you needed to be a good Christian girl all the time.

"Not with him."

"Girl, spill!"

I sighed. "Rox asked me if I needed an emergency call yet, and when I told her I thought I was being stood up, she told me to come to Eileen's."

"The hockey bar?"

I nodded.

"Okay, so..." her eyes widened as the realization dawned on her. "Holy shit, you fucked a hockey player!"

"Kei!" I whined.

"Good for you."

I grimaced.

Her face fell. "Oh no. Was it bad?"

"No. I guess it was okay, but..."

"But you didn't get yours?"

I shook my head.

"Did you say anything?"

I gave her a blank look.

"Maxine! If you're silent, dudes think you're enjoying it."

"I wasn't silent."

"Max! Faking it's not helping your problem. Stop feeling ashamed of liking sex and ask for what you want. Look, I know your parents did a number on you, but sex is healthy. It's okay to like sex."

I rolled my eyes.

Keiana was all about being sex and body-positive and always harped on me about it. Sex made me so uncomfortable. I couldn't even think of the word 'orgasm' without feeling a lot of shame and guilt about it from my strict religious upbringing. I liked sex when I was in the middle of it, but afterward, the guilt sunk in. It was a hard feeling to rectify. Why did something that felt good fill me with such guilt and shame?

"Max, when was the last time you had an or—"

"Can we please not talk about this?" I asked, cutting her off and rubbing a hand over my face.

Keiana nudged my shoulder. "Girl, come on."

I sighed. "With another person? Not since Charlie."

Keiana pulled me into a warm hug, and I melted into her embrace. "Oh, Max, you know he would have wanted you to be happy."

"I know."

"It's not your fault."

I nodded again, but I didn't believe her. "I know, but I'm exhausted, so I'm gonna go to bed."

She didn't let me go. "Who was it?"

I tried to wiggle out of her grasp, but the girl was strong. "Kei, please."

"Tell me!"

"Don't judge me."

She let me go and lifted her hands up as if in surrender. "No judging from me, ever. You know that."

"Yeah, yeah, I know. It wasn't terrible. He was a good kisser. I think he wanted to go for a second round."

"Why didn't you? Maybe he would have gone down on you."

I wrinkled my nose at that. TJ Desjardins was a jerky hockey player, and there was no way he liked doing that. I wasn't even sure if I liked that being done to me. None of the jerks I slept with before ever offered, even though they expected me to go down on them.

"Better to be one and done," I told her.

"Okay, but tell me who it was."

I sighed. "TJ Desjardins."

Her dark eyes were saucers.

"I said don't judge me!"

She tipped her head back in a laugh. "The one who asked for your number and never called you?"

I gritted my teeth. "Yes."

"Damn, girl, he's kinda fine. Not Benny or Mac fine, but he's pretty to look at."

"Benny's very much taken by my boss."

She laughed. "I know. They're like the hottest sports

couple in all of Philadelphia. Too bad TJ was a disappointment."

I shrugged. "I better get to bed. I have work in the morning."

"Sorry about the date, but glad you got laid, even if you didn't get yours."

"S'okay."

She fixed me with a glare. "It's not, Max. Even if it's a hookup, tell them when something isn't working for you. You shouldn't be afraid to speak up."

I gave her a sour face before heading up to my room. I knew Keiana was only trying to help, but I wasn't good at expressing my needs. I never have been; that was just my personality.

I wasn't sure the problem was TJ. Maybe it was me. Maybe I was one of those women who couldn't come from penetration. It felt good when he was touching and kissing me, but when he was inside me, I froze up. Maybe I could only get there if I loved the person. I didn't have that problem with Charlie. Maybe it was because, like always, it reminded me of Charlie, and I felt guilty.

As I was changing for bed, I heard my phone vibrate in my purse. I took it out and checked the screen.

UNKNOWN: *Hey, it's TJ. Can you let me know you got home, okay?*

That was sweet of him, but on the other hand, it annoyed me. Guys like TJ only wanted one thing, and I already gave it to him. So why did he even care?

I knew exactly what it was when I went home with him tonight. I knew I was just another notch on his bedpost. Tomorrow night, he'd probably have some other woman in his bed. That was perfectly fine. I wasn't under any illusions that I was different for him. So why did he care if I got home, okay?

I texted back a one-word answer.

ME: *Home.*

I set my alarm, plugged in my phone, and got under my covers. When I fell into dreamland, I dreamt of my dead boyfriend. I woke up with guilt wrapped around my throat.

My heart still belonged to Charlie, and I didn't deserve happiness when he was dead. Why did I have to survive when he didn't?

CHAPTER FIVE

TJ

"Come on, boys, pick up the slack!" Coach LaVoie yelled from the other end of the ice as he punished us for a loss with a bag skate.

Man, I hated bag skate. Now I felt bad my dad and I made Benny do it when I found out Benny was dating my sister. He deserved it, though. He should have known better than to break the code.

I pumped my legs, trailing behind the big left-winger in question. Benny, Noah, and I played on the same line together, but last night, Coach changed up the lines. Me, Mac, and Hallsy didn't click as well. We all fell apart, leaving Metzy to pick up the pieces guarding the net. Our defense was looking like shit, too, and Riley and Jonesy weren't connecting right. There had been trade rumors about Jonesy lately that had been messing with his game.

I hadn't been playing my best. I dropped so many passes last night, and couldn't find the back of the net. I even got into a fight, which pissed off my sister because she worried about me getting unnecessarily injured. Gotta love her... even when she was a pain in my ass. Not like I was gonna tell her *why* I fought that clown.

My sister was a curvy woman, and guys liked to chirp me about her weight on the ice. They were even worse to Benny about it because he was dating her. I needed to learn to ignore that stuff, but that was my sister, and nobody talked shit on her. We didn't need that penalty, and it was probably why we lost the game. The guilt of letting down my team weighed on me.

The team raced around the ice at practice, all of us huffing and puffing until Coach finally gave us a water break. Coach LaVoie was pretty level-headed. He could be a hard-ass like most coaches, but he wasn't an asshole.

Noah nudged me as I took a drink from my water bottle. "What's with you lately?"

It had been a couple of weeks since I took Max home with me, and I hadn't stopped thinking about her. Or the fact I didn't make her come. I knew I shouldn't care. I should move on. I should bury myself into meaningless sex like I always did. But the idea of taking home a puck bunny wasn't appealing anymore.

I couldn't get the petite blonde out of my head. I wanted to say it was because of my bruised ego, but there was something about her that had her running miles in my brain.

"Nothing," I muttered.

Noah raised an eyebrow at me. Being on the same line as someone—eating, sleeping, and seeing their junk way more than their girlfriend—meant you knew when a guy was bullshitting you. Noah knew when I was lying.

"Bro, what's up? You've been playing like shit lately!" he said.

He wasn't wrong.

"Yeah, man, what gives?" Benny chimed in.

As weird as it sounded, I didn't want to confide in these two. I'd honestly rather ask my sister for advice. Even though Rox would laugh in my face, she would give me excellent advice. Unlike these two knuckleheads.

Riley skated over and sprayed us with ice. "We gotta watch extra video."

I shared an annoyed look with Noah, who rolled his eyes. Riley loved his stats and watching game tape. He was so annoying about it.

"Are you vying for a coaching position or what?" Benny asked him.

Riley poked Benny with a stick, and the two tousled on the ice. Noah peered at me, waiting for me to say something.

"It's nothing," I lied.

"BOYS!" Coach bellowed. "Back to center ice!"

We all groaned and got back down to business. We spent the rest of practice going through our usual drills. I was beat after it, but I couldn't just take a quick shower and head home. After our showers, Coach had us in the media room watching hours and hours of game tape. Riley probably wanted to bust a nut over all the stats. Weirdo.

Coach released us with a warning to get a good night's sleep with no funny business. But instead of driving home, I drove to the arena where the offices were. I needed to talk to my twin.

It shocked me last summer when Rox told me she was moving to Philly. It annoyed me she hadn't told me she was applying for jobs in the States, let alone for the hockey team, but I had to admit I was glad she moved here. Even if she could be a real pain in my ass.

When I walked down to the sales wing, her office door was closed, and I heard the muffled sound of her on the phone.

"She's in a meeting until four," a feminine voice cut in.

I turned to spy Max sitting at her cubicle with her eyes on her computer screen. She wouldn't even look at me.

My gaze roamed down her body, and I saw she was wearing a tight dress that accentuated all her features. My dick jumped against my zipper, remembering how good she looked with her clothes off.

I glanced at the orange flowers on her desk. "What are these?" I asked.

"Tiger lilies," she said flatly. She didn't look at me, just kept her eyes glued to her computer screen.

Ookayyy. She definitely had no desire to see me right now. It made it obvious to me that our night together hadn't been that good for her. I felt like an asshole. It bothered me that instead of telling me, she faked it. I wondered if she was the first woman to do that with me. I always wanted the women I took to my bed to have a good time; I prided myself on that.

"Are you mad at me?" I asked.

She picked up her phone. "Sorry, I'm really busy."

A part of me wondered if she really needed to make a phone call or if she was trying to get me to leave. With a sigh, I walked back down to the parking lot and got into my Maserati.

My sister chirped me for being flashy in my sports car, but I worked my ass off my entire life to make it to the league. When I inked my first big contract, my Maserati was the first thing I bought. Dad drilled into me that a hockey career could be a gamble. Lots of guys made it to the big leagues and blew all their money on cars, women, sometimes even blow. That wasn't me, though. I knew better and tried to be smart with my money...but I needed the car.

I stewed in my thoughts on the ride back to my condo complex in Old City. Benny and Noah carpooled to practice this morning, but I had told them to go without me. It probably hadn't been a good idea because now I was alone with my thoughts.

I wasn't good at being alone. My thoughts got too loud in my head, and they constantly reminded me I wasn't good enough. That I would be alone forever. That's what my ex, Nat, always told me. She played with my heart, so as soon as we cut ties, I became the guy who was never serious, only out for a good time.

But I wasn't sure I wanted to be that guy anymore.

❄

"Stop moping!" my sister said as she barged into my room hours later.

I wrenched my head up at the commotion she was making. "Dude! What the fuck?"

She stomped over to my bed and hovered over me. "Don't 'dude' me! Benny told me you needed to see me. And then Max said you came by while I was in a meeting."

I grimaced.

She narrowed her eyes. "Okay, I don't like that look. What did you do?"

Did I mention my sister was an asshole? God, I loved her, but she was a pain.

I put my pillow over my head and screamed into it. I pulled it away and glared when I saw my sister was still in the room, giving me an annoyed look.

"Go away, Roxie! What if I was fucking beating off, and you walked in?"

"Wouldn't I be able to feel it? Since we got that twin-telepathy?" she growled out sarcastically.

I didn't think that was how it worked. I hoped not. Gross. It was bad enough I found out she was dating Benny by coming home and hearing them going at it. They were loud as fuck. I still think my ears were bleeding from it.

She sat on the bed next to me. "What's wrong with you?"

"I'm in a bad mood," I lied.

"Yeah, no fucking shit! You've been playing like absolute garbage. I've never seen a worse pylon out there."

"Fuck you, Roxie!"

"Eat a dick, hoe!"

"Fucking slut!"

Then we both smiled and cracked up. That was just the way we were with each other. My sister got under my skin, and I got under hers, but she was my best friend.

"Tell me what's going on," she urged again.

I sighed and scrubbed a hand across my jaw. "I have to ask you something super personal."

"Okay..."

Maybe I should have asked Noah or Benny this question instead. I chewed on my lip and looked up at the ceiling as I thought of how to ask her this question.

"Oh my God! What?" she asked.

"Have you ever, you know...faked it?"

"Faked what..." She trailed off, and her features softened as she put two and two together. "Oh. Oh, bud. I'm sorry."

"I feel like I did something wrong, and when I saw her today, she couldn't wait for me to leave."

At that last part, Rox narrowed her eyes. "Goddamnit, Tristan. I specifically asked you not to fuck my employee!"

"She's an adult!"

My sister sighed. "I know, but Max isn't like you."

"What's that supposed to mean?"

"Look, Max is kinda fragile, okay? I love you, and I want you to be happy. I want you to find a love like I have with Benny. But..."

"What?" I snapped.

She peered at me, staring down at me with hazel eyes that mirrored my own. "Do you want that? You've been telling us for so long you don't want to be tied down. You want that bachelor life forever."

It wasn't that I didn't want to settle down. It was just that I didn't think I deserved that.

I knew I should have been over the things my high school girlfriend said to me, but her words still cut deep. I forgave her for it, but when I was alone with my thoughts, her words came back to haunt me. Deep down, I always thought she was right. I didn't deserve what Noah and Dinah had, or what Riley and Fi had, or even what my annoying sister and Benny had. I wasn't like them. I wasn't good enough for anyone, and I never would be.

"It was nice to have someone who cared about me last year. I really fucked up with Taylor," I admitted.

"Wait, a second. Last summer you told me there was someone you were interested in, was that Max?"

I nodded.

I never told Rox I asked Max for her number because I knew it would piss my sister off. Especially since I was a dick and never called. I didn't deserve a good girl like Max, and I certainly didn't deserve love.

"I fucked it up," I said.

"How?" she asked.

"I asked for her number and then never called her."

Hazel eyes bored into me, and then Rox punched me hard. "Ow! What the fuck!"

My twin had a meaner hook than some dudes on the ice.

"Why did you do that?"

I leaned my head back against the wall. "I don't know!"

She narrowed her eyes. "Tristan..."

I changed the subject back to my original question, before she sussed out the thoughts in my head. "Why would she have faked it, though?"

Rox sighed. "I don't know, but some women don't come from penetration alone. Maybe that's all it was. It might not have been something you did."

"You've never done that?"

She shook her head and then stopped to ponder it for a moment. "With Lisa."

"Really?"

She nodded. "A couple of times. She was kinda selfish in bed. Not with Benny."

"Never?"

"Nope!" the big man in question called out. I looked up and saw him standing in the doorway of my bedroom.

He smiled at my sister, and she looked at him like he was her sun and stars. I never thought they would look at each other like that. When I left for Russia last summer, I thought I would come back to my sister being arrested for murder since she hadn't exactly liked the big guy for several years. But now they were disgustingly in love. I pretended it made me sick, but I was glad Roxie found someone who loved her the way she deserved.

"You know your sister. She likes to tell everyone what to

do," Benny said with a dopey grin on his face. Damn, he was so weak for her.

"You like it!" she teased.

His grin got bigger. "You know I do, angel."

Barf. I wanted to get away from all this lovey-dovey stuff. It was so bizarre to see them this way.

Benny gave me a cocky smirk. "Besides, I usually go down on her if I'm not making her come with my dick or fingers."

"BENNY!" my twin shrieked.

"EWWWWW! I don't want to know that!" I yelled at him. I really did not need to know that.

Benny laughed and shrugged shamelessly. Rox shook her head but got up and walked over to him. I watched him bend his head and kiss her like they hadn't just seen each other the moment she walked in the door. As much as it pained me to see my sister with one of my teammates, I'd never seen her look at any of her partners the way she looked at Benny.

Rox walked out of my bedroom with Benny, shutting the door behind her.

I laid on my bed and tried to stop thinking about the mysterious blonde. I didn't know why it bothered me so much that Max faked it. She clearly wanted nothing to do with me, and it wasn't like me to be hung up on a chick.

I should have told myself to forget about her. I should have been banging my way through all of Philadelphia, pretending I didn't feel anything. Instead, I scrolled through Max's social media like a creepy stalker. There was something about this woman that called to me.

CHAPTER SIX

MAXINE

It was easy to avoid a man you had a one-night stand with when he was a professional athlete who was on the road a lot. Except for seeing him yesterday when he wanted to talk to Rox. I gave him the cold shoulder and pretended I was busy; it wasn't like he wanted to talk to me.

I knew the score when I went home with TJ, and I had been fine with that.

There was one problem, though—I couldn't stop thinking about him.

I couldn't stop thinking about how he held me in a gentle, yet firm grip. Or how his kisses made me feel alive. I hadn't felt like that in a very long time.

It was better to avoid TJ at all costs. TJ didn't want something more with me. Besides, I didn't deserve to feel for anyone else what I had felt for Charlie.

Charlie had been the love of my life, and a love like that only comes around once. You only get one soulmate, and I found him as a teen. When my mother found out Charlie and I had sex, she told me God would punish me for my sins. I thought she was being unreasonable, but then a drunk driver hit our car after coming home from graduation. When I was the only one who survived, it made me feel like she had been right.

I didn't deserve to be alive when they weren't. I didn't deserve any happiness. So thinking about the 'what ifs' with a guy like TJ Desjardins was a waste of my time. I'd just avoid him until he gave up on me. I was pretty sure he'd already had multiple women in his bed since me. He wasn't a guy who lingered on one woman. Everybody knew that.

God, or the universe, or even the hockey gods, weren't on my side today though, because when I got into my car after work, it wouldn't start.

"Crap," I swore under my breath and got out of the car.

I popped the hood and looked inside, but I didn't know what I should look for. I had just gotten an oil change, so it couldn't be that. Did I leave my lights on? Was it the battery? I heard loud rap music from a car driving by, but I didn't pay attention to it because my mind was running a mile a minute, trying to figure out why my car was dead.

"Hey! You need a jump?" yelled out an all too familiar voice.

A voice I had been avoiding.

Oh no!

Of all the people to spot me stuck in the arena parking lot, it had to be the one man I couldn't stop thinking about. And the one I was actively avoiding at all costs.

I cursed silently to myself but didn't turn around. "No, I'm fine. Um...just checking something!"

I heard the car pull up in the empty spot next to mine and the engine cut. I turned and watched TJ Desjardins get out of his shiny black Maserati. He looked ever the hockey player in that backwards baseball cap, Bulldogs sweatshirt, and tight jeans. Hockey players and their backwards hats. I swear it was like a law that they always had to wear them. I had to admit, though...he looked good.

He walked over to me with his brow furrowed. "You okay?"

"No!" I snapped.

His hazel eyes widened at my harsh tone, and I felt like a jerk. "You try to turn the key?" he asked.

I sighed and put my hands on my head. I felt them shaking, and I was breathing a little too hard right now. Crap, I felt the pressure of a panic attack coming on. I didn't need this right now. It was bad enough I had a panic attack in Rox's office a month ago and ended up telling her my whole sob story.

"It's a push to start," I muttered.

I heard my heart beat loud in my head and nothing else. I squeezed my eyes shut and tried to breathe, but I was breathing too hard, too much.

No, please. God no.

My palms were sweaty, my chest felt tight, and everything in my head felt *too* loud.

Suddenly, his hands came over mine and pulled them off my face. "Hey, Max, look at me. Breathe, okay?" he asked me in a calming voice. His calloused hands rubbed mine soothingly, and I felt comforted by his touch almost immediately. I hated myself for that. "Can you breathe for me?"

My car was dead and the man I had been avoiding came riding in like he was my obnoxious knight in a shiny sports car. This was just my luck.

"Maxine, it's gonna be okay. Breathe with me, okay?

Listen to my voice," he urged.

I nodded and did as he asked. Slowly, my chest stopped heaving, and my breathing went back to normal. TJ cupped my face, and I couldn't help but remember how he had gingerly cupped my face when he kissed me.

"Are you okay?" he asked, his voice hitching up in concern.

I nodded and pulled away from him but refused to look him in the eye. "I'm sorry you had to see that."

He tilted my chin up to look at him. Worry etched across his face, and when his thumbs brushed across my cheeks, I realized I had been crying.

Great! I had a panic attack over my car dying in front of one of the hockey players. Specifically, the one I never wanted to see again. Why was this my life?

"Hey, talk to me. Are you okay?" he asked again.

"I get panic attacks when I'm overwhelmed," I explained.

"Oh, Max, it's gonna be okay. Let me help you."

I shook my head. "It's fine. Maybe it's my key fob. Why are you at the arena anyway?"

"Rox forgot her skates and needed it for her game tonight. Come on, I'll give you a jump."

I sighed, because clearly he wouldn't give up. It wasn't like I knew what I was doing, anyway.

"Fine," I said in defeat.

I rubbed my hands down my arms and tried to get my body back to normal. I hated having panic attacks, and I hated that I had one in front of him.

I watched TJ go into the trunk of his car to grab the jumper cables and a rectangular item I had never seen before. "What's that?" I asked.

"Jump box," he said like I knew what that meant. He

connected the cables to the box and then to my car battery, then turned to me. "If I jump start your car normally, it could fry your electronics. Since you have a newer car, it's better to use a jump box or call a service. Fate must be on your side that I saw you today. Get in the car and try the button."

I did as he asked, sliding into the driver's seat with my key fob still in my purse, sitting on the passenger's seat. As soon as I pushed the button, everything went back online, and I raised my hand in triumph at the sound of my engine starting.

From my position, I saw TJ take the cables off the battery and shut the hood of my car. He came over to the driver's side door, and I pushed the button on the door to lower the window. "Thanks for your help," I said sheepishly.

He smirked, and the corner of his lip went up to one side of his face. He looked so boyishly cute with that lopsided grin. "I know how you can repay me."

I groaned inwardly. I felt like he was about to ask me to go down on him or sleep with him in the backseat of my car. That was something a cocky hockey player would say.

He leaned on my car. "Let me take you to dinner?"

"What?"

"Dinner, Max," he said again.

"Why? Shouldn't I take you to dinner to thank you?"

He took his hat off and ran a hand through his hair. It reminded me of how good it had felt to run my hands through those silky, dark locks.

"Because I messed up before," he admitted.

"Huh?"

"I should have called. I was a chicken. So let me make it up to you by taking you to dinner."

I stared at him, open-mouthed for a moment. He was asking me out? But why? He already had me in his bed. Guys like him only asked women out so we'd put out.

"That's unnecessary."

I felt awful when I saw the crestfallen look on his face. "Why not?"

"You don't need to do that because you feel bad we slept together. I don't need you to buy me dinner."

"That's not why I'm asking. I want to take you out."

I shook my head. I shouldn't get my hopes up with him. He was only doing this because he felt sorry for me. "You don't need to. I'll buy you a drink later."

I pushed the button to roll up my window, and he stepped back from my car. Watching his disappointed face as I drove away made my stomach ache. He looked upset that I rejected him, but it was best for both of us.

Keiana was home when I keyed into the house after getting groceries for dinner. She worked nights at the hospital, and sometimes I forgot which days she was on. I usually took care of dinner and made sure she had a plate for when she got home. It was the least I could do for all she did for me over the years.

"Hey," she greeted me while she helped me unload the groceries. "What's wrong?"

"I had a panic attack today."

"Max!" she cried and pulled me into a big hug. Kei gave the best hugs. "You okay?"

I nodded. "My car died."

"Why didn't you call me?"

"TJ gave me a jump."

"Really?" she asked, a big grin on her face.

I rubbed a hand over my face. "It was so embarrassing. I don't want anyone to see me like that."

"What happened?"

"He calmed me down, but then..."

"What?"

"He asked me out."

"Wow! See! Maybe he needed a little kick in the pants."

I frowned at her. "I said no."

"Why? Girl, that man's hot. Go out with him. Make him work for it—and ask for yours this time!"

I shook my head. "I think he felt sorry for me."

"Max! I think you should give him another chance."

I shrugged. "He just wants sex."

"Okay...and would that be terrible?"

I shrugged and tried to get her to forget the conversation while I started boiling water for pasta.

"Max?"

"Hmm?"

"I love you, honey, but I think you need to consider seeing someone."

"To date?" I asked.

She shook her head. "No. You never talked to anyone after the accident, and living with this undiagnosed anxiety isn't good for you."

"I'm fine, Kei," I insisted. Talking about your feelings with a stranger wasn't something that was done in my family. I hated even talking about it with Keiana. There was no way I would do that with someone I didn't know.

She frowned but let the argument drop as she helped me in the kitchen for dinner.

I kept thinking about what she said, though. About TJ, not the therapist thing. Maybe I had been cruel to reject him like that. Maybe I should have given him a chance. But I was pretty sure I slammed the door on that today, so I wasn't sure why I was still thinking about it.

CHAPTER SEVEN

TJ

I stormed into the locker room and threw my helmet into my cubby. For the third game in a row, I couldn't set anything up, and the team was in another skid. So much for the home opener win. I didn't want another shitty season under my belt; I wanted to bring the cup back to Philly.

I'd like to blame it on the fact we found out Jonesy got traded to Carolina right before the game started. He had been lacing up his skates, about to go out for warm-ups, when Coach came over to tell him he was in the wrong locker room. But our last two games had been more or less the same. We just weren't clicking out there on the ice together.

"T..." Noah trailed off.

I fixed him with a glare while I ripped off my jersey. Despite our slump, Noah had been playing the best he ever had. He was the only player on the team to get a goal in the past two games. Dude's been on fire. I didn't know what it was, but he was the only one showing up on the ice. Except for Metzy. Metzy kept getting the silver bucket after games because he was a brick wall in front of our net.

I scrubbed a hand over my face and took off the rest of my gear. I hated losing at home. Philly fans were no joke, and they'd tell you when they weren't happy with you. You got used to the boos when you played in this city.

Coach came into the locker room with a grim look on his face. He definitely wasn't happy with us. I wasn't happy with my team or with my playing either.

Coach sighed. "Boys, that wasn't the outcome we wanted tonight."

I slumped down in my cubby and hung my head. I knew it was a team effort to fuck it up, but I felt the weight of failure on my shoulders.

"I expect better of you. All of you." His steely grey eyes fixed on me for a moment, but then he moved onto our captain G. "But tomorrow's another day, so rest up tonight because we're having an early practice."

None of the guys whined and complained about that because we all knew we deserved the punishment. We probably had another bag skate in our future, too.

Coach left, and G took to the floor. "Boys, early practice tomorrow, but I know we could all use a drink, okay? Unless you have a good reason, we're wallowing at Eileen's."

I undressed the rest of the way and took a shower, but my mind was focused on all the shit I did wrong in the game. I was putting my suit back on when I saw a text from my sister.

ROX: *You okay?*
ME: *Fuck no!*

ROX: *I can feel it.*

ME: *BS!*

ROX: *Okay no but Benny told me you're in a bad mood. I'll meet you at the bar.*

I shoved my phone in my pocket and stormed off. Benny strolled along behind me. We carpooled to the game, so it wasn't like I could go anywhere without him.

Tonight was the kind of shitty night where I wanted nothing more than to bury myself into a one-night stand. To find relief in a woman that I would never see again. The problem? I couldn't stop thinking about the petite blonde who turned me down. I shouldn't care. I should be banging bunnies left and right like usual, but every time the occasion arose, I wasn't interested in chicks who looked at me with dollar signs in their eyes.

I climbed into Benny's SUV and scrolled through Max's social media.

"Dude, stop cyberstalking her!" Benny laughed while he pulled out of the parking lot.

I ignored him and continued scrolling.

A gorgeous girl like her wouldn't give me the time of day. I really messed up. I should have asked her out from the get-go instead of being an asshole and ghosting her. I should have taken her on a date before taking her to my bed. She made it clear she wouldn't give me another chance. It wasn't like I deserved it. I should find a bunny to fuck all my angst into tonight. Find a warm body to make me forget all about her.

"T," Benny sighed as he found a parking spot. "What's with you?"

"I don't know, man!"

He cut the engine and gave me a hard look. "Bro..."

"What?"

He sighed and rubbed a hand across his neatly trimmed beard. "You've made it known you fuck chicks and never call them back. I'm not judging you. That's who you are, and the chicks you take home get that."

I scowled. "What's your point?"

"Why haven't you slept with someone since Max? And why are you creeping on her social media all the time?"

I banged my head against the headrest. "I don't know!"

"Bud, figure your shit out because you looked like garbage on the ice tonight."

"I don't deserve her."

Benny narrowed his eyes. "Who? Maxine?"

I nodded. "I don't deserve anyone."

Benny paused and looked at me with pity in his eyes. Dammit, I didn't want my teammates to look at me like that. "TJ, who told you that? Who told you don't deserve someone to love you?"

"Forget it, man. I need a drink and a quick lay to forget about it," I said and got out of his SUV.

Revealing my darkest secret to my teammate wasn't something I ever wanted to do. The only person I let myself be real with was my sister, and that was because she knew me better than anyone.

I walked over to the bar and ordered a lager, hoping my sister would distract Benny so he wouldn't ask any more questions. I looked over and saw her with her legs wrapped around his waist and her tongue in his mouth. As gross as it was, I was glad because my sister kept him from nagging me.

When I turned back around, I came face-to-face with a pretty blonde, but not the one I wanted to see.

"Taylor, hey," I said.

My ex gave me a friendly smile. "Hey, T. Rough game tonight."

I sighed. "Don't remind me. You want a drink?"

"I'm good. Just trying to cash out."

I loosened my tie a bit. "How've you been?"

She gave me a polite smile. I knew I broke her heart, and I felt like a dick about it. "Good. Things are great. How about you?"

This was the most awkward conversation ever.

"Awful," I muttered.

She gave me a pitying look and squeezed my arm. "You'll figure it out. It's still early in the season."

The bartender finally came over and gave me my beer while Taylor asked to cash out.

"It's not that," I said and rubbed a hand over my face.

"What's wrong?"

I sighed. "Can I ask you something personal?"

"Okay..." she said but looked unsure.

The bartender came back with Taylor's credit card receipt while she waited for me to explain.

"Did you ever fake it?" I asked.

She gave me a quizzical look. "Fake what?"

"You know...with me?"

Her brown eyes widened in recognition, but then she vigorously shook her head. "No. T, I knew what you were like when we started hooking up, but you never failed in that department. Did that happen to you?"

I nodded. "Why would she do that?"

She shrugged. "Some women can't come. She might have been afraid of hurting your feelings."

I nodded. That was sort of what my sister said, too, but it didn't make me feel any better. I knew I definitely shouldn't be having this conversation with my ex, though. Especially after I was such a colossal dick to her.

I rubbed the back of my neck. "Look, I'm sorry about everything. I—"

She held up a hand to stop me. "Don't. You made it clear you didn't want anything serious, and I tried to change you. I made my peace with that."

I chewed on my lip. "I'm still sorry. What if I decided I want what you wanted?"

She frowned. "Not gonna happen, TJ. We're over."

I shook my head, but I didn't immediately respond because a flash of blonde came into my peripherals, and I spied the source of my infatuations across the bar talking with my sister. Taylor's gaze shifted to the direction I was looking in.

"Oh," she said quietly in recognition. "You didn't mean me. Who's that?"

I picked at the label of my beer. "Doesn't matter. I fucked up, like I did with you."

Her eyes widened again. "Ohhh. I see."

Maxine locked eyes with me, but then she narrowed them as she studied Taylor standing next to me.

Taylor gave me a quick side hug. "Good luck, TJ."

"I'm still sorry about what happened between us," I said.

She gave me a small smile. "T, I'm happy with Brian." She held up her hand where she had a petite diamond on her ring finger. Whoa, that was fast. "Very happy. I don't think you were ready, and that's okay. You're worthy of love, even if you don't think so."

In a flash, Taylor disappeared.

I never told her about the things Nat said to me, so I

wasn't sure how she knew what I felt like deep down. It wasn't like Rox told her either. Rox had been indifferent to Taylor. Probably because she knew I never got serious with anyone, so it was a waste of her time to get to know my conquests.

That made me sound like such a douche-canoe. No wonder Dinah called me a lovable douche to my face. I kinda deserved it.

I looked over at Max, who was still chatting with my sister. She said something to Rox and then rolled back her shoulders and strolled over to me. My eyes couldn't help but scan down her body. She was wearing a comfy-looking sweater and tight black jeans that made her ass look amazing.

I gave her my signature lopsided grin as she walked up to me. "What brings you here?"

She ignored my question. "Who was that?"

I waved her off and took another sip of my beer. "My ex."

Her eyes softened, and she uncurled her hands from the fists they were in. Huh, that was interesting.

"Okay," she said.

I raised an eyebrow. "Okay, what?"

She looked like she didn't want to answer my question. "Okay, you can take me to dinner."

"Really?" I asked, my voice going up an octave.

She nodded. "But I'm a vegetarian, so if you take me to a steakhouse, it's game over."

"Okay, I'll think of a nice place to take you."

"After your road trip."

"Right."

I forgot I was heading out on another road trip tomorrow.

"Text me!" she said, and then she left as soon as she had appeared.

I wasn't sure if that had actually happened until I was crawling into my bed a couple of hours later and saw a text from her.

BABYGIRL: *I'm serious, somewhere VEGGIE friendly. NOT like I can eat the house salad.*

I felt like that was a sore spot for her. I wasn't about to tell her I had been a creepy cyberstalker, and I already knew she was a vegetarian because she posted something about the vegan fast food place she liked when they opened a new location near the arena.

ME: *Anything for you, baby girl.*

BABYGIRL: *[eye roll emoji]*

I flipped over to my last message with Dinah.

ME: *Hey, stop fucking Noah for like a minute and help me out.*

D: *[laughing face emoji] He fell asleep! What do you want?*

ME: *Aw! You wear him out!*

D: *Fuck yeah I do!*

I had to laugh at that. I loved Noah, and he was one of my best friends, but his five-foot-two girlfriend was the one in charge in that relationship. D didn't give a fuck sometimes, and that's why I loved her.

ME: *You used to be a vegetarian, right? Where's a good place to take a vegetarian girl for dinner?*

D: *ooh...hmm maybe, Greenery? That's kind of fancy.*

D: *Wait, DATE?!?*

ME: *Thanks, D!*

D: *Dick! Gimme the deets!*

ME: *Night, D!*

D: *DETAILS MAN!*

I ignored her last message and started making a plan.

Greenery looked fancy, but it would be perfect. I really needed to impress Max if she was giving me a second chance. I didn't know why she was doing it, but I wanted to make sure I didn't mess it up this time. Something about her made me want to try. Made me want to prove to myself that I wasn't the useless jock everyone thought I was.

CHAPTER EIGHT

MAXINE

"You look nice today," my boss said as she breezed into the office after coming back from the fifth meeting of the day. When I found out we hired TJ Desjardins' sister, I had some concerns, but Rox is incredibly competent.

I smiled and fingered my black skirt. "Is this skirt too short for work?" I asked.

Rox shook her head with a laugh. "No, girl. I'm telling you that you look hot in that outfit. Especially those thigh-high boots. What's the occasion?"

I frowned. "Oh, um...I have a date."

Her hazel eyes sparkled, and her plum-colored lips eased into a smile. "Oh, really?"

"Yes, really," I grumbled.

"With anyone I know?" she teased.

Like TJ hadn't told her. Rox let it slip before that her twin was her confidant, and they told each other everything.

I glared at her. "Like you don't know."

She laughed. "Fuck yeah, I do. FINALLY! I reminded him to go somewhere vegetarian-friendly."

"People always forget! But I told him that was the only condition."

"Yeah, but you also don't speak up about it. I love you, girl, but sometimes you need to tell people how you feel. Especially men."

She had a point. I could be timid and shy. In my last performance review, she told me I wasn't aggressive enough at getting sales. I wasn't very good at asking what I wanted. I was raised to anticipate men's needs above mine, and it had been a hard habit to break.

Sometimes it amazed me I liked men based on the sexist rhetoric my parents fed me. But despite the way I had been treated before, I loved men. I loved a man's rough hands on me while he held me in place and feeling his scruff scraping against my face when he kissed me.

And now I was daydreaming about kissing TJ while talking to his twin sister, who was also my boss. What the heck was I doing?

Rox snapped her fingers in front of my face. "Hello, earth to Maxine!"

I shook my head. "Sorry. What were you saying?"

She smirked. "Oh my god. Were you daydreaming about my brother?"

I was sure my face was crimson red. "Shut up, no. Get out of here! I have cold calls I need to make before I leave for the day."

The smirk stayed firmly on her perfectly made-up face as she went back into her office. I couldn't focus for the last couple hours of my workday because TJ was picking me up for dinner here, and I was nervous. So nervous, I'd had to reapply deodorant three times already. I was trying to tamp down my anxiety, but I was on the verge of another panic attack.

Would TJ kiss me again? Would we end up tangled in the sheets tonight? He didn't exactly please me in bed last time, but maybe this time, I could work up the courage to tell him what I wanted. Anxiety built up in my chest at all the what-ifs swirling in my head.

Before I could start freaking out, the sound of footsteps approaching my cubicle distracted me. When I looked up and saw TJ standing in front of me wearing an impeccably tailored suit and holding a bouquet of tiger lilies, all my frantic thoughts melted away for a second.

He brought me my favorite flowers. I hadn't even told him tiger lilies were my favorites when he asked about them on my desk. My heart did a backflip at the sweet gesture.

He smiled at me and handed me the flowers. "These are for you."

I took them from him and placed them on my desk. "Oh, T, you didn't have to bring me flowers. Thank you, they're my favorite."

His lips quipped up in a grin. "I know."

I cocked my head quizzically. "You do?"

"You had them on your desk when I came by to see my sister. And then I asked her to confirm."

"Really?" I asked.

That was really thoughtful of him, and it surprised me he even thought of it. Maybe I had misjudged him too harshly.

He reached out and tucked a tendril of my hair behind my ear. His hand lingered on my cheek, and I loved the feeling of his big masculine hand on me. "Anything for you, baby girl."

I rolled my eyes. "Okay, none of that. Geez, does that work on the other girls?"

He smirked at me. "Maybe, but it seems to annoy you, so that makes it fun."

I shook my head at him and stood up to grab my coat off the hook outside my cubicle. He surprised me again when he held it open for me and helped me into it.

We walked out to his car together, and he opened the passenger door of his Maserati. I never thought party boy TJ Desjardins could be such a gentleman.

I drummed my finger on the dashboard while he was shutting the door and running around to the driver's side.

"What do you want to listen to?" he asked once he sat down and started the engine.

"I don't care," I said with a shrug.

"Sure..." He trailed off, not at all convinced, but he turned up the volume on some top 40 station.

Honestly, I didn't have the heart to tell him I didn't listen to music. I spent most of my commute listening to either true crime podcasts or audiobooks. Secular music wasn't allowed growing up, so when I got to college, I had no taste and listened to whatever was playing at the parties I ended up at. Thank God for Keiana. I wouldn't have survived UPenn if it wasn't for her.

At a red light, I felt his eyes on me, and I looked over to catch his gaze trailing up my skirt. My cheeks felt hot. "You look nice," he said with a naughty grin because he knew I caught him.

"Thank you," I muttered meekly. I eyed his classic black suit. "Am I underdressed?"

He shook his head. "I'm not sure. D said this place is kinda fancy, but you always look good."

"Noah Kennedy's girlfriend?"

He nodded. "She used to be a vegetarian."

A smile curled up on my lips. "You asked her for advice?"

"Maybe..."

"Are you trying to impress me?"

He grinned. "Maybe..."

He looked so cute with that naughty grin that I couldn't help but keep the smile on my face. It eased my nerves that he was trying to impress me. Maybe that meant he was a little anxious, too. He probably didn't have a panic attack this morning like I did when I asked Keiana what to wear, though.

It wasn't long before we reached Center City, and he pulled his car into a parking garage. We were in the nicer part of the city, and I had a good idea where he was taking me.

TJ came around to my side of the car to open the door for me. I took his offered hand and let him slip his fingers in between mine. He absent-mindedly rubbed the pad of his thumb across the back of my palm, and I felt my breath hitch. TJ was a surprisingly touchy guy, and there was something deep inside of me that was doing cartwheels because of it.

"It's not a far walk," he said while he pulled me onto the sidewalk with him.

"So where are we going?"

"Dinah recommended Greenery. Have you been?"

I looked up at the old historic brownstone in front of us. It was a pretty nice restaurant, so maybe I *was* a little underdressed. I had been dying to try this restaurant, but it was pricey. Damn, TJ had done well.

"I haven't been, but I've been wanting to."

He beamed. "Score!"

I laughed at that. He was adorable, especially with that smile aimed at only me. He only let go of my hand so he could open the door for me. Since he had a reservation, they showed us to our table right away. TJ helped me with my coat and even pulled out my chair. This gentleman TJ was not the one I had a one-night stand with, but I liked this side of him.

The server took our order, and TJ waited for me to make my selection before asking if I wanted wine. He didn't assume what I wanted, and my heart flipped over in my chest that he was letting me make my own decisions.

I sipped my wine and glanced over at him from across the table. His face was clean-shaven tonight, which I loved, but his five o'clock shadow was already coming in. He didn't seem like a man who could grow a lot of facial hair, but I was okay with that. I preferred the clean-cut look.

"Why did you insist we go to dinner?" I asked.

"I felt bad about what happened between us."

I cocked my head at him. "How so?"

He shifted in his chair uncomfortably. "I shouldn't have asked for your number and then ghosted on you."

"Can't ghost me if you never called."

He grimaced. "I'm sorry. About everything. I shouldn't have done that."

"It's okay, T. This more than makes up for you forgetting my number."

"I hope so. I definitely should have bought you dinner before I took you to bed. Maybe that's why you didn't..." he trailed off and rubbed the back of his neck.

I knitted my eyebrows as I tried to figure out what he was going to say. We locked eyes, and the pained look on his face told me everything.

He *knew* I faked it. I thought I was so good at faking it!

At least I never had any complaints before. Usually, men didn't care if you came as long as they did.

"You know I faked it?" I asked in a low whisper. I felt my pulse beating faster as anxiety coursed up through my body. This was certainly not where I wanted this conversation to go.

"Yeah, I could tell," he said, and a dark shadow came across his face.

I looked down at the table and couldn't look him in the eyes. Why did I have to be so awkward about this? Why couldn't I have asked him what I wanted?

Oh, right, because sex made me feel guilty.

"I'm sorry," I muttered.

"I hope I didn't pressure you into doing anything you didn't want to do. I feel like I messed everything up."

"You didn't force me to do anything, okay?"

"I know my sister tried to ward you off of me, telling you I'm not a relationship guy, which used to be true...but I think I want something more."

"Oh."

He grimaced, and I felt like a jerk. This man was baring his soul to me, and all I could say was 'oh.'

"I'm sorry. 'Oh' probably isn't what you want to hear. I'm just surprised. I figured you got me into bed and then you could move on. I didn't think you were looking for something more."

He gritted his teeth but shook his head as if shaking it away. "I haven't had a serious relationship since high school."

"I...neither have I."

"She messed me up," he admitted.

My heart broke for the man across the table from me. I

knew there had to be something more to him. He wore a mask to hide his insecurities, just like me.

I reached out a hand towards him, and he smiled at me. "TJ, I'm so sorry."

"You didn't do anything wrong, baby girl."

I rolled my eyes at the cheesy nickname. "Ugh! You're insufferable."

He gave me that grin again, and I shook my head at him but laughed and relaxed into his company.

CHAPTER NINE

TJ

I smiled at Maxine over the top of my wineglass. I preferred a good beer, but I discovered there were some wines I enjoyed. My sister hated wine, and in our quest to find one she liked, I found my own preferences. Rox still hated wine, but it made me seem all cultured and shit with the ladies.

I really wanted to impress Maxine and make-up for my fuck-ups. She seemed cagey when I told her I was looking for something more than a hookup. I noticed she didn't say she wanted that too. Maybe I was coming on too strong, but there was something about her that made me stop looking at anyone else in the room.

Especially tonight. She looked good enough to eat, especially in those thigh-high boots. Holy fuck, I wanted to know what it felt like when the heels dug into my back while she wrapped her legs around me.

I needed to slow my roll. I wanted to take whatever this was with Max, slowly. I wanted to make sure she knew I was for real and not just looking for another quick lay. She deserved better than how I treated her.

"So, why did you go into sales?" I asked.

She shrugged. "I wanted to work for the team. I love hockey."

"Okay, I get you're from Philly."

"Born and raised. South Philly represent!"

I laughed. "Dinah's from South Philly."

"I didn't know that. Where at?"

I shrugged. "How am I supposed to know that?"

"Some friend you are. We don't know each other, though. Well, I know she's Noah Kennedy's girlfriend, but I've never met her."

"Really? Even though you're both from South Philly?"

She shook her head with a laugh. "I don't know everyone who lives in South Philly! But I also went to a fancy private school."

I raised an eyebrow. "Oh?"

"Yeah, that's why I'm so friendly with the bartender at Eileen's. The Holmstroms went to the same school."

Ah, that would explain why the bald-headed bartender glared at me when Max was around. Maybe he had an old flame for her or something.

"Did you grow up vegetarian?" I asked.

She frowned and took a sip of her wine.

Shit, how was that the wrong question to ask? I couldn't back-pedal because then our food came. For vegan food, it wasn't half-bad, but I would be hungry later.

"I'm sorry," I said.

"Don't be. I grew up in a very strict household," she said and took a bite of her food.

Oh, that might explain why she was so reserved.

"Do you have siblings?" I asked.

She shook her head. "Nope. I'm an orphan, though."
Oh.
Oh, fuck.
I hit the biggest nerve a guy could hit on a first date. What was wrong with me?

"I'm sorry," I said again.

Christ, I sounded like Noah. I wasn't a guy who apologized. I wasn't a Canadian stereotype like my buddy was.

She wrinkled her cute little nose. "For what? You weren't the drunk asshole who killed my parents."

Rox mentioned Max rarely swore and usually got embarrassed when my sister did it in front of her. Rox swore worse than any hockey player in any locker room I'd ever been in. The poor girl had to put up with a lot, with Rox being her boss. That Max was swearing meant I obviously struck a nerve.

How did I keep on colossally messing up with her?

"Max, I'm—"

"Can we talk about something else?" she interrupted me.

"Sure."

"Like...what are you doing out on the ice right now?"

I groaned.

She gave me a playful smile. "What? After that home opener, you ran out of gas."

"I didn't know you were such a hockey fanatic."

"I bleed black and red! But seriously, what gives?"

I shrugged.

I couldn't tell her I was pretty sure the reason I was looking so sluggish on the ice was that I couldn't stop thinking about her. For once in my life, instead of being the guy who moved onto the next girl, one had stuck with me.

Or maybe it was because Coach kept switching up the lines because none of us were clicking right.

"I don't know," I sighed and took another bite of my eggplant braciole.

"I love LaVoie. He was my childhood crush—"

"I'm gonna tell him you said that," I teased.

"Don't you dare!" she squealed.

I gave her the famous Desjardins smirk, and the grin on her face got bigger. I liked getting to know this mysterious woman. I'd rather she razz me about how shitty I was playing instead of upsetting her like I had when I brought up her parents.

"Anyway!" she started back up again and gave me a playful glare. "I don't understand why he keeps separating you from Noah and Benny. Your line works."

"I'll tell Coach you have some thoughts."

She laughed. "No!"

I smiled at her from across the table and watched her shovel another forkful of grilled tofu into her mouth. She closed her eyes and moaned. My dick twitched behind the zipper of my dress pants at the sound. She definitely hadn't made that sound when we were together. That sounded like a genuine moan, and I wanted to hear it once I had her beneath me again.

But not tonight. I had to make it up to her first.

"Good, eh?" I asked.

She smiled while she swallowed her food. "I'm sorry. Are you going to be hungry again?"

"Max, it's okay. I'm a big boy," I said and took another bite of my dinner.

We had ordered stuffed avocados as an appetizer before our entrees, but she was right—I would be hungry later. I'd live. Especially since I knew there was leftover pozole in the fridge from last night. Living with Benny definitely had some benefits. He was an awesome cook, and he always made enough food as if he was cooking for the entire team.

I took another bite of my dish. "Our captain, G, switched to plant-based after he had a baby."

Her eyes sparkled with interest. "Really?"

"Yeah. His diet's mostly rice, oats, fruits, vegetables, and whole grain."

"So no tofu?" she asked as she took another bite of her own meal.

I cocked my head as I thought about when he tried to convince me to go plant-based. "I don't think so. Sometimes salmon if we have a big win and we go out for a team dinner, but that's rare. Some of the older players are going plant-based more so they can extend their careers."

"That's interesting. Have you ever considered it?"

I shook my head. "I think I'd get too hungry."

She laughed, and I smiled at her from over my glass. I was so glad the awkwardness of bringing up her parents had passed. As far as first dates went, this one was going pretty well. Or at least I hoped it was. There was something about Max that made me want to peel back all her layers and get to know her better. That made me want to make this the perfect first date.

After we finished dinner, we ordered a figgy vegan cheesecake dessert to share while I sipped on a coffee. I understood now why she freaked out about me driving her home the night we slept together, so another glass of wine was out of the question. I didn't want to be out too late tonight anyway, since we had a game tomorrow.

After we finished, I paid the bill, even though she tried to argue with me. I secretly loved it when women did that.

But I made a shit-ton of money playing hockey; I could afford to take her to dinner.

I helped her into her coat, and I took her hand when we walked outside. "Where to?" I asked.

She didn't miss a beat. "My place."

I grinned, and we walked back to the parking garage to get my car. In hindsight, maybe it should have been better to take a rideshare, but I would know that for next time. I knew what she meant when she said, 'my place,' especially with the way her eyes had been tracking over me all night. She wouldn't get it that easy, though. Not this time.

She gave me her address, and I drove across town to South Philly to a brick facade row house.

"Oh, I know this neighborhood," I said.

"Oh, yeah?" she asked.

"Yeah, Metzy lives not that far away."

"Oh! Right! We went to the same prep school."

"Small world."

I didn't cut my engine because I wasn't coming inside with her. She turned to me, and I leaned across the center console. I pushed her hair behind her ear and slanted my mouth on hers. She made a little noise in her throat, but then she kissed me back, and her tongue slid across the seam of my lips. I smiled into the kiss and let her take the lead, letting her set the pace as she deepened the kiss. We tangled together, and I slid my hand through her silky blonde hair while I pulled her closer.

A few minutes later, she pulled away and was out of breath. Her blue eyes were wild with a hunger I had only seen a glimmer of the last time I kissed her. "Are you coming in?" she whispered huskily.

Oh, she definitely wanted it, but I needed to play it slow

with her. I caressed her cheek with the back of my hand. "Not tonight."

Her face fell. "What? Why not?"

"We should take it slow."

She glared at me. "TJ, please come upstairs and..." She trailed off, all flustered.

I got the feeling talking about sex was uncomfortable for her. I wanted the next time we were together to be something we could discuss and explore together. We jumped too soon before. I had been a horny bastard, and the next time I had her, I wanted to savor every last inch of her. I wanted her to beg for my dick after I made her come multiple times.

"And what?" I asked, giving her my famous smirk again.

Her cheeks colored. "We can...you know."

"What?"

She growled at me. This tiny five-foot-five woman actually growled at me. Hell yeah, I wanted to get her there, but she wasn't ready yet. I had already fucked up with her so many times; I needed to take it slow. I needed her to know this wasn't just a casual thing for me. That I was ready to stop being the guy who slept through all of Philadelphia.

I shouldn't want that. I should want to have as many girls in my bed as I could. Maybe my sister was right, maybe losing Taylor was a wake-up call.

"You know. We can have sex," she muttered and clenched her teeth.

I faux-gasped. "I don't put out on a first date!"

She shook her head and laughed. "Seriously? You? We already had sex."

I brushed her hair behind her ear. "Patience, baby girl."

"I had a great time," she said.

"And?"

She gave me an exasperated look. "I'd like to do it again sometime."

"Okay."

She squinted at me. "You're really not gonna come upstairs?"

I laughed and shook my head. "Don't tempt me. You gotta earn this hot bod."

She laughed again, a sound that had my dick perking up behind my zipper. That was going to have to wait. She unbuckled her seatbelt and leaned over to plant a quick kiss on my lips. "Are you serious?" she asked when she pulled away.

I nodded and cupped her face. "I want to take it slow."

"Why?"

Because I didn't deserve her, because *I* was the one who had to earn it, to make amends for being a douche to her. Because she was the type of woman you savored.

"Just because, baby girl. Be patient."

She gave me an annoyed look. "Fine."

I gave her another chaste kiss goodnight. "Night, baby girl."

"Night, T."

She pulled away slowly, and it killed me to watch her get out of my car. My dick was throbbing as I watched her walk away. Yes, I watched her ass in particular. I was a guy, so of course I noticed that. But taking it slow was the right course of action. I could always use my hand on myself when I got home. I didn't want to jump into bed again. With Max, I needed to prove I was worthy of her.

She waved when she got to the doorstep, but I idled in my car, making sure she got into the house okay. I waited a few minutes before I took off and headed back to Old City.

When I walked into my condo, I noticed my roommate's

door was shut, which wasn't unusual, but I heard voices murmuring behind it. I took off my shoes and was loosening my tie when Benny's door opened. The big man walked out of his room in only a pair of boxers. His dark eyebrows raised at the sight of me.

He grinned and called back into his bedroom, "Angel, you owe me fifty bucks!"

I shook my head at him. My sister never used to like her partners calling her pet-names, but somehow he got away with it. Rox appeared in the doorway, wearing one of Benny's shirts.

I wanted to barf because I knew what that meant.

Her eyes widened. "What are you doing home?"

"Why? Am I being a cockblock?" I joked and went into the kitchen to get a glass of water.

Benny laughed, and Rox slapped him on the shoulder. He hugged her from behind and whispered something in her ear. It amazed me they were so in love now, because months ago they would have been screaming at each other. I guess love was funny like that.

"No," Rox said. "But I know Max's roommate works night shifts, so..."

I shook my head. "Nah. I don't put out on the first date."

Benny laughed. "Okay, sure, buddy."

My sister narrowed her eyes at me. "Really? You?"

I shrugged and ran a hand through my hair. "Yes. Plus, I might have struck a nerve tonight."

My twin's face fell, and she crossed her arms over her chest. "What did you do?"

"She told me about her parents."

"Oh...I'm sure you didn't completely mess it up. Does she want to go out again?"

I ran my thumb over my bottom lip, thinking about the

hungry look in Maxine's eyes before she asked me to come upstairs. "Oh, most definitely. We have to earn it, though."

"Whoa..." Benny exclaimed. "You really like this girl, huh, T?"

I nodded. "Yeah, but she's still a mystery to me."

Benny kissed my sister's temple. "Yup, I know all about those mysterious girls. Did you invite her to the game tomorrow?"

I stared at them for half a second. "Should I?"

He shrugged. "That's what I would have done."

I bit my nail and looked at my sister for guidance.

"Tristan, don't worry about it. You'll figure something out. Now, if you excuse me, I'm sweaty and gross and need a shower before going to bed."

I stuck my tongue out at her. "Gross. I didn't need to know that."

She flipped me the bird on the way into Benny's room. He was not subtle about watching her ass as she walked away. I flicked him on the ear. "Hey, that's still my sister. Gross!"

He grinned at me. "And she's my girlfriend! Who would have thought?"

"Definitely not me, bud."

CHAPTER TEN

MAXINE

"What do you mean you didn't get laid?" Keiana screeched at me with righteous indignation.

I was lying on the couch in our living room, waiting for the Bulldogs game to start. Keiana had gotten off shift a little while ago and ran upstairs to sleep until she smelled the coffee I made.

I shrugged. "He said he didn't put out on the first date."

I was still mad about that. TJ Desjardins didn't have sex on the first date? I felt like I was in a parallel universe because that didn't compute at all.

I had such a great time with TJ last night, and I thought he wanted me beneath him again. It surprised me when he refused to come inside. Wasn't that the reason he had asked me out in the first place?

Keiana flipped her black box-style braids over her shoulder. "Are you serious? You already slept together!"

"I know! Ugh, I was so mad at him. I even invited him up, and he said I had to earn his hot bod."

She cackled. "Oh my god, he did not say that!"

"Yes!"

She walked over to the couch and sunk into it next to me. She put my feet in her lap as she drank her coffee. "Well, I'm happy that you at least asked for what you wanted. That's a start!"

I sighed and flicked my gaze to the TV where the puck was about to drop.

I wished I wasn't so awkward about sex, but when your parents shamed you into thinking sex was a bad thing, it was hard to shake those feelings. Sex always made me feel bad about myself and guilty. Maybe it was because those other guys weren't Charlie. Keiana thought I needed to have an emotional connection to someone to enjoy sex, and maybe she was onto something. I hadn't felt guilty about what I did with Charlie — until it had cost him his life. I would always blame myself for surviving, even though I hadn't been the drunk driver who killed him and my parents that night.

Keiana poked me. "Hey, stop going inside your head; puck's about to drop."

"How was work?" I asked, changing the subject. I turned back to the TV and watched our team captain Girard lining up for the puck drop.

She shrugged. "Exhausting. It's a living, though."

I nodded.

I was glad TJ didn't ask about my job all that much during our date. Since his sister was my boss, it wouldn't have been smart to talk about it. I loved working for the team, but sales wasn't exactly where I wanted to be. I wasn't particularly good at it, but leaving the team wasn't an option for me, and I didn't know what I wanted to do instead. It wasn't like I could go into Rox's office and say, 'hey, I don't like this job you pay me to do; can I have another one?' It was a good job, and it paid my bills, but I definitely hated what I did. That wasn't something you said to someone who was intimately close with your boss. If I told TJ how I really felt about my job, I worried he'd tell his sister. They told each other everything, after all. I couldn't jeopardize my career like that.

I watched Girard get possession of the puck, and when I saw number 76 skating across the ice open for the pass, I jumped. TJ took the puck from Girard and then quickly passed it to Noah, who lobbed it towards the net.

I groaned when it went off the pipes.

"Bullshit!" Keiana yelled next to me.

"Tough break. They'll get it together," I said, but I wasn't sure I believed it myself.

Philly fans had two speeds — cocky or distraught. Lately, we had been on the distraught speed, especially with our hockey team.

Last year the Bulldogs had an awful season, and even though they were only a few weeks into this season, I had my doubts. I kinda felt like a jerk with how I razzed TJ about his playing last night. He hadn't seemed offended, though; he just laughed it off. The team needed to get out of their current skid. St. Louis won the cup last year, and at one point in the season, they were legit the worst team in the league. So it didn't matter how you won the cup; you just had to get there first. I would die if I ever got to see my team hoist the cup again.

The doorbell rang, which was odd since no one ever came over unannounced. Keiana pushed my legs off of her lap, and she went to answer it. I heard her talking to whoever was at the door, but then she shut it, and I didn't hear anyone else come in.

"Who was that?" I asked, not taking my eyes off the screen.

"Um...I think it's for you," she said. Her voice was a little muffled.

I turned around and saw her holding an enormous bouquet of tiger lilies. My eyes were saucers.

She laughed and walked into the kitchen. I sprang up from the couch and followed her into the other room. She put the vase on the table, and I picked up the card from off the bouquet.

I had a great time last night, baby girl. Can't wait for our next date. You tell me the time and place.

~TJ

"When did he have time to do this?" I asked.

Keiana smirked and peeked over my shoulder. "Oh, that boy's smooth as shit. Baby girl?"

I rolled my eyes. "I think he calls me that because it annoys me."

She laughed. "It's cute!"

"It's annoying!"

She elbowed me. "You totally like it."

I tried to hide my smile. There was a tiny sliver of me that liked it, but I'd never admit it. I didn't have time to argue with her because the sound of the goal horn and the crowd yelling on the TV distracted me. I heard my phone buzzing on the coffee table, so I knew we missed something exciting.

I walked back into the living room and saw the score ticker reading, T. Desjardins (76) assist - N. Kennedy (13) and A. Halls (44).

Crap! I missed TJ's goal!

"What happened?" Keiana asked as she walked back into the living room.

"Missed the first goal of the game. It was TJ's."

She beamed at me. "He sent you flowers."

I swatted her away. "He also brought me flowers yesterday. They're at my desk at work."

She raised a dark eyebrow. "No shit?"

I nodded.

"When was the last time you went out with a guy that did romantic stuff like that?"

Um.

Never.

The fifth of never.

All the guys I slept with since Charlie's death hadn't been serious or were one-night stands. Not like there were that many.

Keiana nudged me.

"Never, Kei. I think Charlie brought me flowers on our first date...but you know I haven't had a boyfriend since him."

Her mouth was a thin line. "So TJ's not the douchey hockey player we thought, huh?"

"No, he is, but he said something about his ex messing him up last night. I think he wants something more with me."

That was what scared me the most. What if he only thought he wanted something more? I didn't want to get my hopes up with him because everyone knew he wasn't a relationship guy. My heart kept yelling at me to give him a chance since he was a complete gentleman last night, and then he sent me flowers. My favorite flowers. Men never remembered small stuff like that, and it pulled at my heartstrings.

I texted my boss instead.

ME: *Did you have a hand in your brother sending me flowers today?*

ROX: *...what? No! He did that?*

ME: *YES. Also, the holding penalty they just called on him was BS!*

ROX: *Oh...Max, I think my brother actually has feelings. I always thought he was a robot.*

ROX: *I heard you told him about your parents.*

ME: *It slipped out.*

ROX: *Charlie too?*

ME: *NO.*

ROX: *I didn't think so, but I didn't say anything. You should have come to the game today! Meet us at Eileen's for drinks after!*

ROX: *PLEASE!!!!*

MAX: *Ugh, you're annoying, fine.*

I got up from the couch with a stretch. Keiana eyed me curiously. "What's up?"

"Rox wants me to meet her for drinks after the game."

Her brown eyes twinkled. "Oooh...fun!"

"You want to come with me?"

She shook her head. "Nah, I'm on shift tonight, gonna go back to sleep for a little while. Have fun, don't do anything I wouldn't do."

I walked up the steps so I could go get a shower. I needed to be presentable if I was going to see TJ again tonight. Even if it meant I missed part of the game. I showered and dressed in my cutest long-sleeved sweater dress. With the thigh-high boots again, because I wasn't completely clueless. I saw the heated look TJ gave me whenever he saw me in these boots.

When I came downstairs, the third period of the game

was halfway over, but Keiana wasn't around, so she must have been asleep already. I sat down on the couch and finished watching the game. Miraculously, they won.

My phone buzzed with another text from Rox.

ROX: *Change of plans, come to my brother's condo in Old City!*

ROX: *I'm making him order you a car.*

I didn't know where tonight was going, but I was excited. I didn't want to get my hopes up, though, because TJ had let me down before. But maybe having some sexy fun with him would finally get me over my issues in the bedroom. It didn't have to be serious. Maybe being with the hockey playboy could help me stop feeling so shameful about sex.

CHAPTER ELEVEN

TJ

My sister bounded across the room and opened the front door. My breath caught in my throat when I saw Max walk in wearing a black sweater dress that hugged her lean body in all the right places and those boots again. Those fucking boots! Did she know I liked them so much? Because she seemed to always wear them around me. She slipped them off at the door while she and my sister talked.

What was she doing here? Not that I was complaining. Seeing Maxine in my condo after we won a game was a good sign.

I gave my sister an annoyed look, but she pretended not to see it as she led Max to the couch. Max took the seat next to Benny, who gave her a smile and said hello.

I took my hat off and ran my fingers through my hair, trying to smooth it down. If my sister told me she was inviting Max over, I wouldn't have changed into a plain t-shirt and jeans after the game. I probably would have stayed in the monkey suit, if only to impress her.

Man, what was with me? I never let chicks get me this nervous. I didn't know what it was about Maxine that made me want to be good enough for her.

I realized I didn't have any wine, so I took out my phone and texted Dinah.

ME: *Any chance you have wine?*
DINAH: *I'll ask Noah to check.*

Seconds later, Noah opened the door to my condo with a bottle of merlot in his hand. He handed it to me with a smirk on his face. I grabbed two glasses from the cabinet and poured a generous amount into both. I swatted Noah's hand away when he tried to swipe the glass.

"Not for you," I said.

He laughed and ran a hand through his long hockey flow. "I saw Max's here. Rox's doing?"

I nodded.

"Did she like the flowers?"

It had been Noah's idea to send flowers to Max after our date with a note. I shrugged. "Not sure yet."

He pushed me towards the living room. "Well, get over there and talk to the lady already."

Max's eyes lit up when she saw me, and I handed her the glass of wine. "Oh, you didn't have to do that," she said sheepishly.

I situated myself in the armchair next to her. "No problem."

She took a sip of the wine and tucked a strand of blonde hair behind her ear. Next to her, my sister and Benny cuddled together and spoke in hushed whispers.

"Oh, thanks for the flowers. You didn't have to do that,"

Max said. She stared blankly into her wineglass and wouldn't look me in the eye.

Max was such a mystery to me. I didn't normally go for the shy woman, but I felt like she was coming out of her shell last night. Now it felt like she had gone back inside, and I didn't like that.

"Glad you liked them," I said with a smile.

I felt my sister's eyes on me, and we had a telepathic conversation.

Benny glared at me. "I wish you two would stop doing that shit."

Max looked between the two of us with a confused look. "What?"

I shrugged. "Twin intuition."

Rox scoffed and rolled her eyes. "That's made up, and you know it."

I shook my head. "It's real, and you know it. I felt awful that day you got that concussion."

This was an argument we would have on our deathbeds. Rox didn't think twin intuition was real, but I knew it was. In her last year at the University of Toronto, she had a nasty spill on the ice and ended up with a concussion. That same day, I felt weird all day and played the worst game of my career. When I got the call about her accident on the ice, I realized why.

Max sipped on her wine silently as she observed me and my sister having a stare-off.

"Hey, are you hungry?" I asked her.

She nodded.

"Come on. I'll take you to get something to eat."

"Smooth," my sister and Benny mouthed behind Max's head.

Max smiled at me. "Can I finish my wine first?"

I laughed. "Absolutely. Unless…you do dairy, right?"

She nodded. "Yes. What are you thinking, pizza?"

"Definitely. Calls for a celebration. We won a game!"

Benny barked out a laugh. "Yeah, that's kind of our job, dude."

I pulled out my phone and placed an order for a couple of pies. Like normal, we had a bunch of people over after a game. Metzy and his girl Lacey were over in the corner chatting up Hallsy and his girl Mia, and two of our rookies were milling about chatting with girls I didn't recognize. If food came, everyone would eat it.

My sister slid off of Benny's lap, and she dragged him into the other room. She did that on purpose to give Max and me some space. I moved onto the couch beside Max and put my arm over the back of it.

"They're so cute," Max said with a small smile across her pretty face.

I ran a hand through my hair. "Ha! You didn't know them when they were at each other's throats."

She gave me a shocked look. "What are you talking about?"

"Oh, they hated each other for years. Actually, I think it was more my sister than Benny."

"Gosh, why? Benny's the nicest guy. I think he and Noah might be in competition for the Lady Byng."

I laughed. "I think you're right. Noah's such a Canadian stereotype! When they first met, Benny took one look at my sister and went, 'holy shit, are your tits for real?' And then they fought like cats and dogs for three years."

She looked at me in horror. "I don't believe you!"

"It's true! I don't think he meant to say it out loud."

She laughed into her wineglass. I loved the sound of her

laugh, and I wanted to keep making that sound come out of her.

"Does this count as another date?" she asked after she swallowed her last sip of wine.

I winked at her. "If you want it to, baby girl."

She rolled her eyes. "Will you stop?"

I shook my head, making her laugh again.

We sat together and made awkward small talk until my phone buzzed with an alert from the front desk about the pizza. I walked over to the door and opened it. I paid the delivery guy and then walked back into the kitchen. I put the pizza boxes on the island and swatted Metzy's hand away when he grabbed a slice of plain pizza.

"Leave the plain for my girl," I said.

Max stood in the kitchen and looked for a place to put her empty wineglass. Dinah plucked it out of her hand and handed her a plate. "Here. Vegetarian?" she asked.

Max nodded. "Five years."

"Nice! I was vegetarian for eight. I'm Dinah—Noah's girlfriend." Dinah put her hand out, and Max shook it..

"Maxine. I uhh—Rox is my boss."

Noah and Metzy both gave me a look, but I didn't blame Max for the confusion. We hadn't put a label on things yet. I wasn't sure if I could do the boyfriend thing, but I wanted to try it with her. It was why I wouldn't go inside with her last night. I had already messed it up so much; I had to woo her a little before I had her in my bed again.

Max daintily ate her slice of pizza and talked with Dinah about their experiences being vegetarian. Noah nudged me with his elbow as we stood next to each other, leaning up against the kitchen counter.

"Stop it," I scolded him.

He smirked. "No, you get a taste of your own medicine now."

"Shut it!"

He laughed.

He was probably right, though. I gave him a lot of grief when he and Dinah were figuring out their feelings for each other.

I poured myself another glass of wine and turned to Max. "Max, you want another glass?" I asked.

"Oh, yes, please."

Hmm, I liked the sound of that phrase on her lips.

I poured her another glass and handed it off to her. I took her empty plate and put it in the dishwasher. I wished I didn't have to get up so early to fly tomorrow. Or I would have been inviting her to stay over tonight.

The girls chatted for a bit while the boys and I started talking shop until some people started heading out. Which made sense since we had to get up early for our road trip tomorrow.

My sister gave me a knowing look before dragging Benny into his bedroom, leaving Max and me alone.

"I should probably get going," Max said, but something rooted her to the spot.

"I wish you didn't have to, but I have an early flight tomorrow."

She nodded. "Sorry if I hijacked your get together."

I shook my head and pushed her hair behind her ear. "Not at all. I'm glad I got to see you before I left. I should have gotten you a ticket to the game."

"You don't have to do that. I like watching from my couch and yelling 'shoot' at you," she said with a cheeky smile.

I laughed. I liked when she came out of her shell to chirp me.

"I should call a car," she said.

"C'mere you," I growled.

I threaded my hand through her hair and slanted my mouth onto hers. She laid her hand flat on my chest while we kissed, our mouths hungry and aching to never let go. Her kisses were timid and shy at first until my tongue glided across the seam of her lips. When she opened to me, it was like she unlocked a part of herself she kept a secret from everyone else. I tilted her head to get a better angle and devoured her mouth.

She made a surprised noise in her throat when I nipped at her bottom lip and clenched her jaw in my hands. She gripped my shoulders while we kissed until we forgot to breathe. Then our hands were desperately roaming over skin. She straddled me while I slid my hands up her bare thighs. I wanted to touch her again; I wanted to taste her, and I wanted her to enjoy it this time. But I didn't want to push her.

I left a hot trail of kisses down her neck, and she tilted her head to give me more access. I smiled into her skin at the tiny moans escaping her lips. My hands had a mind of their own as I played with the string of her thong underneath her dress.

"TJ, please," she moaned.

I kissed up her neck and sucked on her earlobe. "What?"

"Can you...can you touch me, please?" she asked in a shaky voice.

"You sure?" I whispered in her ear.

She nodded. "Yes, please. But maybe not in your living room?"

I laughed and lifted her in my arms while I stood up from the couch. I carried her into my bedroom and placed her at the foot of my bed. I sat down next to her, but before I could lean over and press my lips to hers again, she took my hand and put it under her dress.

I grinned and toyed with her skimpy underwear. "Oh, yeah?"

She nodded and tipped her head up to kiss me again. I gave in to the kiss while my hand dipped inside her panties. "Can I take these off?" I asked in-between kisses.

She nodded but then pulled back to pull her dress off. She looked so good in her matching bra and panties. My mouth actually watered. She reached behind her and unclipped her bra, releasing her assets from their booby-prison. Why were bras ever invented? Free the boobies! I slid her underwear off her and slowly settled her onto her back.

"We can go slow," I reassured her.

"Take off your clothes," she said.

I did as the lady asked. Her eyes looked at me hungrily while I shed my clothes. My dick was as hard as a rock, but tonight was all about her. I owed it to her after last time.

I stretched out on the bed next to her, kissing her again, while my hands roamed down her body. I caressed her nipples and loved the sound of her gasp when my mouth traveled down the length of her body. When I reached the valley of her breasts, I licked one nipple until it was a stark point and sucked it into my mouth.

I lifted my head. Seeing her eyes closed in pleasure was a sight to behold. "Good?"

She nodded, and I continued to stroke her with my tongue, moving to her other breast to give it the attention it needed. She arched her back, pressing herself into my mouth. I dipped a hand between the juncture of her thighs and parted her with my thick fingers. I heard her suck in a breath while I gently caressed her clit.

I barely bothered with foreplay the last time I had her in my bed. Was I an asshole or what?

I lifted my head from off her chest and kissed her neck. "This okay?"

I didn't normally ask at this point of the hookup, but I felt like with Max, I needed to make sure this was okay with her. I needed to know she wanted me to touch her.

"Uh-huh," she moaned.

I stared into her eyes, searching for confirmation.

She nodded. "Please."

"Tell me what you like."

"Getting finger-banged," she admitted, and then a blush crept up her face. She smacked a hand over her mouth like she was shocked by what had come out of it. She looked so cute, embarrassed by her admittance. I liked that she let herself get flustered with me. That she let her sexual side come out.

With my free hand, I stroked her face. "Don't be afraid to tell me what you want. Let me give you what you need."

"I need to come. Please," she begged.

Fuck me, I wanted to get her there.

I kissed her neck while I stroked her clit in a slow circle. "Baby girl gets what she wants."

She made a little whimper, and my dick definitely liked that sound. I would deal with that later. First, I needed to give her all the pleasure she could ever want.

I ran my middle finger down across her slit, gauging her arousal. I slid one finger inside while I nipped at her neck. When she rocked against me, I pressed a second finger inside and moved them in and out slowly. She clenched around my fingers, a reminder of how good it felt being inside her. I wanted that again, but not yet.

She slapped a hand over her mouth, and I grinned onto her neck because I knew that meant she was into it.

"I want to make you come," I whispered huskily. "Can I taste you tonight?"

"You...what?" she asked and looked at me with hooded-eyes full of desire.

I lifted my head from the crook of her neck. "Max, has no one ever eaten you out before?"

The blush spread across her face again, but then she shook her head.

I pulled my fingers out of her and got up from the bed. I couldn't believe no one had ever done that for her before.

I pulled her legs down to the edge of the bed and kneeled in front of her. She was glistening wet and sexy as fuck. I wanted to kiss and lick and suck at her, but I wanted to make sure she wanted that.

I looked up at her. "Seriously, no guy has ever gone down on you before?"

She shook her head. "They always want me to give them oral, but they never return the favor."

"I don't want you to return the favor tonight, maybe later, but tonight, I want to pleasure you."

She gave me a hard look. "I don't believe you."

I sighed. "Okay, I might need to jack it while I do it, but I want to taste you on my tongue. Let me make it up to you for not making you come the last time."

I dipped my head between her thighs and flicked my tongue across her clit.

"Ohhh...okay, proceed," she consented.

"Mmm..." I moaned into her and drawled my tongue across her, tasting her for the first time.

I loved pleasing a woman by going down on them. I loved feeling their thighs clasp against my head and hearing them moan in ecstasy. It was the best sound in the world.

I reached a hand down to stroke myself while I lapped at her center. I licked at her clit and felt her squirm above me. I looked up at her, and she had a hand clamped over her mouth.

"Are you going to come for me?" I asked and nipped at her thighs.

She nodded vigorously and bit her lip. "I don't want Benny and your sister to hear me org—"

She cut herself off and clamped her hand on her mouth again when I wrapped my lips around her clit and gave it a nice, long suck. Her hand wasn't doing much to muffle the sounds, especially when she was grinding her mound onto my face. I continued to lick at her while I stroked myself.

"I don't care. I want to hear your moan, for real this time," I demanded before I let my tongue do the rest of the talking. She was so close, I could feel it, and I wanted to taste her cum on my tongue.

"TJ," she moaned. Now she didn't care if my sister or my roommate heard her whimpering moans. I didn't give a shit either. I wanted to hear her scream my name while I watched her arch her back in ecstasy.

She removed her hands from her mouth and gripped my hair in between her fingers as she rode out the wave of her orgasm on my face. I lapped it up while she ground on my face, all sexy and demanding to get hers. I liked this side of her. The side that dropped her guard and took what she wanted from me. Because there was nothing hotter than watching as I made her come.

I stroked my cock while I moaned into her pussy and gave her some final gentle licks on her sensitive clit. She clamped her hand over her mouth again, but I heard her cry out as she orgasmed. This time for real. It was so fucking sexy, and I couldn't wait until the next time I had her spread eagle across my bed while she came with my name on her lips.

Her face was flushed, and she was panting, but she looked so sexy, naked and sated in my bed. I stroked my cock as I stared at her beautiful form, and it didn't take long before I was blowing my load into my hand.

I stood up to grab a tissue off the bedside table and cleaned myself up.

I crawled into bed beside her. "You okay?" I asked.

She nodded and looked down at my softening dick. "Do you need me to do something for you?"

I shook my head and kissed her forehead. "Nah, I'm all good. Tonight was about you."

"I should go."

"Let me call you a car."

She nodded while she grabbed her clothes and put them back on. She was biting her lip, unsure, while I got dressed.

I stepped in front of her and cupped her face. "You sure you're okay?" I asked.

She smiled, and I wanted to trap that image in my head. Of this shy woman smiling at me like I was the only man in the entire world. Nobody looked at me like that before, and I felt a warm sensation wrap itself around me at the sight.

So I just kissed her again instead.

CHAPTER TWELVE

MAXINE

"*...And it's denied by rookie goaltender Seamus Metz!*" the announcer on the TV above the bar yelled.

I peered up at the screen, but all I noticed was the camera panning to the bench where TJ and Noah sat on it together, chewing on their mouth guards.

The score was 2-1, Chicago, and after losing to Minnesota a couple of days ago, the team needed another win. Next to me, Rox drank her beer and tapped her black manicured fingernails on top of the bar. Her eyes darted back and forth as she watched Benny lining up for the face-off. He got kicked out, and Girard had to take it instead.

"Fuck," she whispered under her breath when they lost possession and Chicago tried to set up a play in the Bulldogs' zone.

It was long-standing that the sales team did happy hour on Thursday nights at Eileen's, but since the game was on, Rox and I stayed later at the bar so we could watch the rest of the hockey game together since the team was still on the road.

TJ and I had been texting on and off since he'd been on the road, but texting differed from seeing him in person. The last time I saw him, he had my body singing beneath his touch. And his tongue, if I was being honest. I hadn't lied when I said no one had gone down on me before. I didn't know if he was actually good at it since I didn't have a baseline to compare. I just knew he made me feel amazing. I might have been daydreaming about it a lot.

Rox snapped her fingers at me. "Hello, earth to Maxine!"

I shook my head at her. "Sorry. What?"

She threw a napkin at me. "Girl, what's up with you?"

"Nothing!" I protested and took another sip of my wine.

She cocked a dark eyebrow at me. "Hmm."

"What does 'hmm' mean?"

She smirked at me. "Have you talked to my brother lately?"

I nodded. "Yeah, he called me last night after they lost to Minnesota. He seemed upset."

"Really? I was wondering why he didn't call me. He normally wants to hash out terrible games with me."

"Uhh...sorry?" I offered.

When TJ video chatted with me last night, I was a little surprised. But then my heart melted the tiniest bit when he said he wanted to hear my voice and see my face. It was sweet but also confusing. We had only been on two dates and weren't exactly dating. Despite his confession that he wanted something more with me, everyone knew TJ wasn't boyfriend material. I kept reminding myself not to get my hopes up.

Rox waved me off with her hand and took another big

chug of her beer. "Don't worry about it. Benny wanted to have a sexy video chat with me, so I didn't want to talk to Tristan, anyway."

I blushed, and she laughed. Rox was so blunt, but I didn't think she did it on purpose.

"Sorry. Does it make you feel uncomfortable when I say stuff like that?" she asked. "I know I'm your boss. I don't want you to feel uncomfortable."

"It's not that. I'm a prude."

She cocked her head at me but didn't ask the question on her mind.

"Sex makes me uncomfortable," I said with a grimace.

"Why?"

I sighed and drained the rest of my wine.

"I grew up super religious. My parents basically shamed me into thinking sex was wrong," I explained. "You're not supposed to like it, and it was only for procreation."

She made a face. "Oh, woof. Your parents would have hated a bi girl like me, eh?"

I laughed. She had no idea.

She put a hand on mine. "It's okay to feel uncomfortable, but you need to be open and honest with your partners about how you feel. You have to trust the person you're with. Even if it's just a hookup. When you have sex with someone, there's a certain level of trust you're giving to that other person. You're giving yourself over to them and letting them see all your sides."

She had a point. The odd thing was, I didn't feel guilty after TJ went down on me. At all. I had been happy and sated, and that was super scary to me. I didn't understand why it didn't make me feel bad about myself. It was like there was something about TJ that made me drop my guard and be okay with giving in to my desires. It both confused and scared me.

I glanced up at the TV again and saw TJ carrying the puck over the blue line with Noah right there with him. He deked around the Chicago defenseman and passed to Noah, who went for the backdoor wraparound goal.

"Fuck yes!" Rox squealed beside me when it went in.

I smiled at her while I watched Noah and TJ celebrating with each other. Hockey players were so cute when they got excited about a goal. Goal cellies were one of my favorite parts of the game.

My thoughts drifted off to TJ again. Maybe he wasn't the jerky hockey player I thought he was. A part of me was still worried, though. TJ was on the road a lot, and he was known for being a no-strings-attached guy. We never said we were exclusive, but that didn't mean I liked the idea of him hooking up with other women.

Rox poked at me. "Hey, where do you keep going?"

I swatted her hand away. "Nowhere. Is it hard doing the hockey girlfriend thing?"

She peered at me for a moment and then sighed. "I won't lie to you—it is. When Benny and I got together, he was around a lot because it was the offseason. It got harder when I started playing hockey again, too, but I'm going to fight for him."

"TJ told me you two hated each other for years."

She ran a hand through her dark hair. "Yeah, I guess I saw what I wanted to see."

"He worships the ground you walk on."

She scoffed. "He does not."

"He so does!"

She grinned. "Sometimes he calls me a goddess..."

I smiled at that. "Oh, my God! That man loves you so much."

She placed her hands on her heart and smiled really big. "Yeah, he does. It took us a bit, though. We snuck around because I wasn't sure it was serious."

"You look happy together. You think he'll pop the question soon?"

She wrinkled her nose. "Gross, no."

"No? Don't you want the whole marriage, kids, and the happily ever after?"

She shook her head. "I have my happily ever after. Not everyone's idea of that means marriage and family. Don't give me that pitying look. Benny feels the same way. Despite the nagging from both of our families."

That seemed like a sad existence to me but to each their own. If that's what they wanted, maybe it worked for them. I wanted marriage and kids...but I wasn't sure I deserved it. I wasn't sure I'd ever find it.

Our conversation shifted back to the game. The team ended up winning, and Rox and I went on our merry separate ways.

Once I got back to my house, I tossed my phone on the bathroom counter while I took a shower. When I got out and checked my phone again, I saw I missed a call and a text from TJ.

TJ: *Hey, baby girl, are you still awake? I miss you.*

My heart thrummed at his message. On the one hand, I missed him too, and this baby girl nonsense *was* growing on me. On the other hand, I worried he was just drunk and horny. I stared at my phone while I blow-dried my hair and thought about if I should respond.

My phone buzzed on the sink again, lighting up with another text from TJ.

TJ: *Can I call you?*

His message confused me. Lately, he had been so sweet that I wondered what the catch was. When would the rug be pulled out from me when he returned to his playboy ways? TJ didn't do relationships. He slept with as many women as he could and never called them back. Where was the guy who did that to me last summer?

I unplugged the hairdryer and got into my bed. I sunk down into my covers and decided to video-chat with him.

He answered right away, his image materializing on my screen in a matter of seconds. He was in his hotel room, his dark hair wet from his shower, and he wasn't wearing a shirt. Of course he wasn't.

"Hi," I whispered.

"Oh no, did I wake you?" he asked, his brow furrowing.

"No. I was just getting into bed. I saw your assist tonight. You looked good."

He beamed at me. "Rox said you went to Eileen's for drinks and watched together."

I nodded. "Yup. Your sister can be a trip, but she's good people."

He laughed. "She can be a bit much, but you gotta love her. I don't want to keep you. I know you have work in the morning."

"It's okay. I can spare a few minutes."

He gave me that cute lopsided smirk that made my knees weak. It was a good thing I was already horizontal. "I wanted to hear your voice again," he whispered.

"Aw, T, you're getting soft on me."

"Don't be a jerk!" he teased, but he grinned again.

"You know, I never gave you a time and place for our next date."

He raised an eyebrow. "Ooh, I get a third date. Lay it on me."

I laughed. "I'll look at your game schedule, and we'll figure out a time." I glanced at the clock and yawned.

"Aw, baby girl, don't let me keep you awake."

I rolled my eyes at the baby girl comment again. "Goodnight, TJ."

"Night, Max."

I hung up with him and laid back in my bed. Was I a complete fool for starting something with a hockey player known for being a player both on and off the ice? My head was screaming yes, but my heart did cartwheels every time we spoke. I wasn't sure who to listen to.

CHAPTER THIRTEEN

TJ

I chewed on my mouth guard and watched as my teammates set up the play down on the ice. Noah was sitting beside me on the bench and also chewing on his mouth guard. We were up 2-1 against Buffalo, but they were hungry for a win. Especially since the game was getting down to the wire. I felt a tap on my helmet behind me, and Coach called for the change-up. I hopped over the bench with the rest of the line and sliced my skates into the ice.

Noah got possession of the puck and carried it over the blue line, while Logan got tangled up with the opposing defenseman. I skated up the other side of the ice, leaving my stick open, waiting for Noah to set up the play. Noah slapped the puck towards me, and the opposing defenseman tried to get it out from under me, but I took the shot and slipped it past Buffalo's goaltender.

Right in the five hole!

FUCK YEAH!

Noah skated over to me and we hugged it out, cellying hard at the game-winning goal. The roar of the home crowd definitely helped, too.

The atmosphere in the locker room was bumping when I walked in and stripped off my jersey. It was nice to have your team behind your back win or lose, but it was awesome when you were greeted with cheers.

I had to speak to the media afterward since I scored the game-winning goal. I was sweaty and wanted to take a shower, but it was a necessary evil when it came to my career. I answered their questions as best as I could and took the quickest shower ever. I was fixing my tie and checking my phone to see if Max had texted me back yet when Noah nudged me.

"You gonna see your girl tonight?" he asked with a grin.

I shrugged. "She's not my girl."

Noah fixed his hair and smoothed down his beard. "Oh, come on. You called her every night on the road!"

"Ooh!" Riley and Benny crooned as if they were one.

Dicks.

"TJ, the man who claims he doesn't want to be 'tied down,' has a girlfriend?" Benny mocked.

I shot him a glare. "Can it, Benny!"

Max said she was going to come to the game with my sister and meet us for drinks later, but I hadn't checked my phone since I got to the arena. I didn't pay attention once I hit the ice. Some guys would wave to their partners or kids during warm-ups, but I got too into the zone. As soon as my skates hit the ice, I tunnel visioned getting the puck to the back of the net.

I ignored my nosy teammates and checked my phone.

BABY GIRL: *Nice goal, hockey boy!*

ME: *Hockey boy?*

BABY GIRL: *Yeah, that's my annoying nickname for you since you have one for me.*

ME: *HA! Will I get to see you tonight?*

BABY GIRL: *Yes, and hurry because my wine is getting warm waiting for you.*

I grinned and put my phone back in my pocket. Noah smirked at me again, but I ignored him as we walked out of the arena together and toward his SUV. We liked to carpool to the game together. Sometimes with Benny too. I think Benny was going to Rox's place tonight, though, because he drove himself.

When I entered the bar, I forgot about my buddy because I saw the cute blonde sipping on a glass of wine and letting my loud-mouth sister talk her ear off. Rox's eyes lit up but not to see me. Nope. She threw herself into Benny's arms, who laughed and kissed her hard on the mouth.

I made a face, but my eyes connected with Max's from across the bar. She was wearing a Claude LaVoie jersey and jeans that hugged her ass. God, I had missed her face. I don't remember if I felt that way with Taylor. Or any of the other hookups I had before Max. Seeing her waiting for me hit me square in the chest.

I crossed the bar to her and gave her a hug. "Hey, baby girl."

"Hockey boy," she teased.

I ordered a beer and sipped on it with a smile. "I think the nickname's growing on me."

She frowned. "That wasn't the point. It's supposed to annoy you."

I pushed her hair behind her ear. "Nothing you call me could ever annoy me."

Her face colored, and I wanted to say it was because of

the wine in front of her, but I knew it wasn't. She gave me a sly smile. "Okay...hockey douche."

I tipped back my head and laughed. "Oh, the girl's got jokes!"

She put a finger on my lips. "Hush, the entire bar's watching us."

"I don't give a fuck!"

She shook her head at me as if it embarrassed her to be seen with me, but the smile behind her ocean-blue eyes told me otherwise.

I missed her while I was on the road. And this woman wasn't even my girlfriend. I didn't know what she was yet, but I definitely didn't want her to be another random hookup. Being alone didn't appeal to me anymore, and the mindless unemotional sex was making me feel empty inside. I saw all my teammates with their significant others; I saw how my sister was with Benny. It was time for me to stop being scared and let myself find love. For real this time.

"That was a sweet goal, hockey boy," she said and took a big gulp of her wine.

I settled myself onto the barstool next to her and took a pull off my beer. "Yeah, it was pretty nice." I pointed at the name on the back of her jersey. "Um...how come you're not wearing my jersey?"

Her eyes twinkled with mirth. "Hmm...I don't think you've earned it yet."

I laughed. "And Coach has?"

She grinned. "Oh, love of my hockey life!"

"I'll be sure to tell his wife that," I quipped.

She smiled back at me but didn't have a retort because Noah and Dinah walked over to us. Dinah smiled at Maxine. "Hi, again!"

Max smiled back at her. "Good to see you. Oh! I read your book this weekend."

Dinah's smile could have lit up a whole hockey arena. "Which one?"

"Oh, all of them," Max said with a shrug.

Dinah's mouth hung open. "Already?"

Max nodded. "I was addicted. I had to know if all the couples were gonna get together. I usually read more adult romances, but I like young adult too."

Dinah beamed. "Oh, my friend Fi, Aaron Riley's wife, is coming out with a super sexy adult romance."

"Oh, I'm game!"

Dinah nodded, and then the two were having a conversation I couldn't keep up with. Although, inside, I was glad Max was getting on with Dinah. Before Noah and Dinah got together, the three of us were tight. Noah shrugged at me, and we started rehashing the game while the girls chatted. It had been a close game, and we really needed to step it up if we were going to make the playoffs this year.

I ordered another beer and noticed Max finished with her wine. "You want another drink, baby girl?" I asked.

She smiled. Behind her, Dinah and Noah mouthed 'baby girl?' at me, but I ignored them. The bartender refilled Max's glass, and I watched her tip the wine glass into her mouth. Her lush mouth that kissed me hungrily the last time I had seen her. Shit, now my dick was pressed up against the zipper of my pants.

Noah leaned down to say something to Dinah, and she laughed. "Hey, you two, we're gonna get out of here. It was nice to see you again, Max."

I hugged them and settled back onto my barstool. My hand went to the back of Max's neck as I played with her hair. She twirled the wineglass in her hand as she sipped it in thought.

"Do you have work tomorrow?" I asked.

She yawned and nodded. "Yeah, sorry."

"Hey, this counts as date number three."

She smiled and drank more of her wine. "Oh, does it now?"

I nodded. "Yeah, I'm ignoring the boys, so I can talk to my girl."

Her cheeks went that cute shade of pinkish-red when she got embarrassed. I never knew I'd be into shy girls, but it looked cute on Max. The more time I spent with her, the more I liked it.

I frowned when I remembered I flew out early tomorrow for another road trip. Yes, another one. We just traveled only to come back home for one game, and then we were back out tomorrow for another road game.

"What's wrong?" she asked.

"I have to fly again tomorrow, and I'll miss you."

She smiled. "It's okay. You'll owe me a date when you get back."

"I'm keeping you to that, baby girl."

"Yeah?"

"Yeah," I whispered huskily as I nuzzled my face into her neck. She smelled so good, like citrus and possibilities. She gave me hope I could be good enough, that I *was* good enough for her.

"TJ?"

"Hmm?" I whispered as I pressed my lips against her neck.

"Are you gonna kiss me now?"

I chuckled and felt it vibrate across her lithe body. I cupped her face in my hands and slanted my lips over hers.

Kissing her after being apart for a week felt like coming home. I didn't know what I was doing with her, I didn't know if I could be enough for her, but I knew I didn't want to be the lonely guy who tried to fill the hole in his heart with casual sex. At least not anymore.

She pulled back but had a smile that lit up the entire room. "There are so many puck bunnies glaring at me."

I smirked at her. "Let them stare."

"Yeah?"

"I'm not doing the bunny circuit anymore."

"No?"

"Nope. Now hush, and let me kiss you properly."

I think she was going to laugh again, but I swallowed it with another kiss.

CHAPTER FOURTEEN

MAXINE

"Kei! Help!" I cried from my defeated position on my bed.

It was Friday night, and I was preparing for another date with TJ since he was finally back in town.

My bestie bursted into my room only to see me lying on my bed still wearing my work clothes. My work clothes weren't bad, but I didn't think dress pants screamed 'sexy' to a guy like TJ. I wanted to impress him tonight. After a few stolen kisses the other night, I needed more from him.

She gave me a pitying look. "What are you doing?"

Keiana was in her scrubs since she was on shift again tonight and would be leaving for work soon. Which meant I had the house to myself tonight. I was definitely going to ask TJ to come in after our date. I wanted him in my bed tonight. That explained my current freak out.

"I don't know what to wear!" I cried.

She raised an eyebrow. "Why are you freaking out? Isn't TJ your man already?"

"No! We've only gone on a couple of dates," I argued.

"Okay, but...he called you after every game when he was on the road last week. He's so your boyfriend."

I shook my head.

TJ and I never put a label on what we were doing. He said he wasn't doing the 'bunny circuit' anymore, but I still had some insecurities that whatever we were wasn't serious.

Keiana rolled her eyes at me. "Max, he wouldn't call you while he was away if he was sleeping around. Stop worrying."

I bit my lip. "You know why I'm freaking out."

I sat up against my bed and wrapped my arms around myself. Keiana understood why sex made me feel shameful, despite her best efforts to help me normalize my feelings. In the end, sex made me feel dirty and awkward, and it made it harder for me to form relationships. I never told men what I liked or initiated sex, and I was nervous that the last time with TJ had been a fluke. He made me let go. But what if that old shame came back tonight?

Keiana put a hand on my shoulder. "Are you afraid you're gonna have sex with him again?"

"Yes," I sputtered. "No! I don't know. But the last time I didn't feel guilty about it, and I guess I'm scared about what that means."

"Wait, last time you faked it. I'm confused."

I put my hand over my face. I hadn't told Keiana TJ went down on me because I knew how she'd react. I pulled my hand off my face, and she gave me the stink eye.

"Explain yourself!" she demanded.

"We hooked up the night Rox invited me over to his condo," I said and looked down at my hands.

"Why didn't you tell me that?"

I blushed. "Because...because he went down on me!"

Keiana knew my track record with jerky men who refused to do oral. Men were such babies sometimes. She smiled at me. "Really?"

I nodded. "And damn, Kei, it was so good. Like I had to put my hands over my mouth so his sister and roommate couldn't hear me moaning."

She barked out a laugh. "Oh, my God! Must have been good if you're swearing."

I kicked her playfully with my foot. I didn't really swear, mostly force of habit from my upbringing. People thought it was so 'adorable' when I swore. "Don't make fun of me!"

"Did you return the favor?"

I shook my head. "He..." I trailed off and made the universal sign for jacking off. "Is that weird?"

"Did you think it was weird?"

I tapped my fingernail against my lips. "No, it was nice. It made me think he was enjoying it so much he couldn't help himself. Like eating me out made him so horny, he couldn't contain it, and he had to come with me."

"How did you feel after?"

The words flew out of my mouth before I could stop them. "Good...but kind of annoyed because I wanted to suck his dick!"

Keiana's mouth hung open, and I clamped a hand over my mouth. I hadn't meant to say what I was thinking out loud. We dissolved into laughter because it was the first time I was open with her about something sexual. Normally, I tried to shut down the topic altogether.

She stood up from the bed and went over to my closet. "Where is he taking you tonight?"

"A speakeasy."

"The one in Chinatown?" she asked as she flipped through my hangers.

"Nah, the one near Rittenhouse Square."

"Nice. For dinner? I don't think they have food there."

I shook my head. "Nah, I ate when I got home from work. That's why we're not meeting until eight."

"Wear the sexy thigh-high boots, your long-sleeve black sweater, and that cute gray plaid skirt," she said. She took the clothes out of my closet and laid them on the bed.

I eyed my boots lying on the floor next to the door. "You know, I think he really likes the boots."

"Yeah?"

I nodded. "He gets a weird look in his eye whenever I wear them."

She laughed. "He's probably thinking of fucking you in them."

"Perv!"

"You love me!"

"I do. Thanks, Kei."

She came over to me and gave me a big hug. "I'm proud of you for being open and honest with me tonight. I don't want you to feel like we can't talk about these things. We can, anytime you want, and you know I believe in the judgment-free zone. Are you gonna invite TJ in tonight?"

I shrugged. "We'll see how the night goes. I don't know if I earned it yet."

She laughed. "I gotta jet, but have fun tonight!"

I watched her rush out of my room and heard the front door slam shut. I changed into my date clothes and was finishing my make-up when my phone buzzed.

TJ was here!

I raced downstairs to find him standing outside my door, waiting for me. He was wearing a nice pair of jeans and a soft-looking navy blue sweater underneath a black coat. He gave me that lopsided grin and greeted me with a kiss on the cheek.

"Hey, baby girl."

I rolled my eyes. "Come on, hockey boy, let's go. Wait, did you drive?"

He shook his head but poked at his phone. A Honda Civic pulled up on the street in front of us, and he grabbed my hand and guided me toward it. He let me in first and then slid in beside me. I felt warmth envelop me at the feeling of his hand sliding through mine when our fingers clasped tightly around each other.

He told the driver where we were going, but my mind was somewhere else.

I gasped when he brought the back of my hand up to his lips for a soft kiss. "Maxine, relax."

"I can't relax! I'm too uptight!" I exclaimed.

He chuckled. "Which is why we're gonna get you a nice drink to calm you down."

He unlinked our hands and put his arm around my shoulder, pulling me into his wide chest. I leaned back into him, feeling safe and secure in his arms. When we got to Center City, he helped me out of the car, and we walked up to a nondescript building with a bouncer standing in front. I fished into my purse for my ID, and TJ pulled his from his wallet.

The bouncer held up a finger and said, "Let me check," before walking downstairs.

I eyed TJ, but he grinned and laced his hand in mine again. The bouncer was back a few seconds later, and he led us down the steps into a dimly lit room with a tiny bar. We sat at a small table with a padded bench across the wall. TJ let me sit against the wall, and he had the seat facing the outside. For a speakeasy, it was loud in here.

TJ furrowed his brow as he perused the menu. "I have no idea what to order."

I laughed and scanned all the weirdly named cocktails. "Something fun!"

"Hmmm, maybe I'll get an old-fashioned. What are you gonna get?"

I stared down at the menu and read through all the drink names and their ingredients. "Hmm...this is called 'Dynamite with a Bang.' It has pineapple juice in it. I think I'll get that."

He wrinkled his nose. "Sounds too sweet for me."

"I like sweet."

The corner of his mouth upturned into a sly smile, but then the server came over to get our order.

When the server came back with our drinks, I took a tiny sip of mine and almost choked. It was super strong, but I felt more relaxed. It was also a little too sweet, so TJ wouldn't like it.

It was dark in the bar, but it was romantic with the lit candles on the table. It was nice to share it with the man sitting across from me.

"How was work?" he asked.

I shrugged and took another sip of my drink.

"That's all I get?"

"TJ, don't tell your sister...but I don't actually like my job," I admitted.

He winked. "Your secret's definitely safe with me. She's explained her job before, and it doesn't sound like something I'd want to do."

"Of course not. You play hockey for a living!"

He reached across the table and grabbed my hand. "Okay, so what's your passion?"

I chewed on my lip as I thought about his question. "I don't think I have one."

"What?"

I shrugged. "To be honest, I don't like the job itself, but I love working for the team."

He sipped his old-fashioned in silence at my admittance.

What was there to say? Being in sales wasn't a glamorous job, and I wasn't that good at it. I didn't want to tell him how much I truly hated it. Lots of people didn't like their job, but sometimes the job actually pained me. I couldn't tell him that I only stayed because I loved that I got to work for the Bulldogs. Who knew if that would get back to my boss. He didn't need to know how I really felt about my job.

"Sorry if I pushed you about it. I wonder what I'll do after hockey," he admitted.

"You're only twenty-five. You still have a long career ahead of you," I argued.

He shrugged. "One severe injury, and it could go to shit."

I squeezed his hand. "Hey, don't think about that. You're still in your prime."

He nodded and swallowed more of his drink. We flirted and talked a bit more, and when I finished my too-sweet drink; he gave me that lopsided smirk again. "Want to get out of here?"

"Yes, please! Let's go to my place."

TJ paid our tab and called up a car again. Nerves shot through me all the way to South Philly. He twirled his fingers into my hair and kissed my neck to help me relax, but I had to keep wiping my sweaty palms on my skirt. He distracted me by pulling my face towards his and capturing my lips in a comforting kiss.

I got so lost in his kiss, I didn't even remember getting out of the car. It was a blur of lips and hands as we made our way to the door. His hands were on my hips and his lips on my neck while I struggled to unlock the front door.

Once inside, I went to kick off the boots when he took off his shoes. "No, leave them."

I raised an eyebrow. "Why?"

"Because they're sexy, and I want to fuck you in them."

My heart went all the way to my stomach, and I was sure my face was crimson. TJ ran a hand down my cheek. "Too much?" he asked.

I shook my head, but stammered, "N-no..."

He cupped my face. "Hey, if you're uncomfortable, we don't have to do anything tonight."

I shook my head. "No, it's not that. It's just..."

"What?"

I groaned. "Sex makes me uncomfortable."

TJ frowned. "Max, do you not like sex?"

"No! That's not what I'm saying. It's..." I ran a hand through my hair. "It's hard to explain. I grew up super religious, so I'm kind of repressed. I always feel ashamed afterward."

His face fell. "Oh, Max, I'm sorry. Did you feel that way after we had sex?"

I looked down at the boots on my feet. "Yes."

He tilted my chin up so I'd look him in the eye. "Aw, baby, I'm sorry."

"It's not your fault. I thought it was a one-night stand, but now..."

When he stared back at me, his hazel eyes burned into my very soul. "Tell me."

"I didn't feel bad after you went down on me. It felt amazing."

"You want me to help you feel good again?"

I grabbed his hand and dragged him up to my bedroom.

He smirked at the show of aggression as I pushed him down onto my bed once we were in my bedroom. He sat on the edge of the bed, and I sank to my knees in front of him. "I want to make you feel good, like you did for me."

I unbuckled his belt and pulled down the zipper of his pants. I felt his hard length thickening at my light touch, but he removed my hand. "You sure?" he asked.

I reached inside his boxers and touched him instead of answering.

He hissed at the sensation but grabbed my wrist. "Take off your clothes."

"You first."

He grinned and shed the sweater, flinging it somewhere on my floor. Ugh, I forgot how cut he was. He was like a work of art. I ran my hand down his abs, and then I pulled his jeans and boxers down over his thick thighs.

I dipped my head down towards his cock, but he pulled me back by my hair and looked at me sternly. "Keep the boots on, but I want to see you naked when you're on your knees."

I gulped. I liked that demand.

I shed my sweater and unzipped my skirt. His eyes scorched across my body, taking in the black push-up bra and matching lacy thong. He pulled me down to straddle him and kissed me hard. I leaned into the kiss so much I didn't notice he undid my bra until it was sliding down my chest and his hands were caressing my breasts. He kneaded them and pinched my nipples into hard, aching points.

His hands skated down my back, and he cupped my bare ass. "You're a little vixen, eh?" he whispered into my ear. He played with the string of my thong, just barely grazing the soft skin I wanted him to touch.

"T…" I whined. "I want to taste you."

He nipped at my earlobe. "Okay. But only if you want to."

"I want to."

"Then get on your knees."

I kissed him hard again, and I moaned into it while I ground in his lap. I loved his hands holding me in place and his hardness beneath me. When I was with him, I didn't feel that old guilt, and I just wanted to let the pleasure take hold. It was like being with him let me drop my guard and stop worrying about the things my parents had drilled into me my entire life.

I moved off him and took my time slipping the thong off. I was naked, sans the thigh-high boots, and TJ looked at me like I was a three-course meal.

"Get over here," he growled.

I liked this demanding alpha-male stuff, but I wouldn't let him know that. I sunk onto my knees and nuzzled his hardness against my face. I felt his hands grasp my hair, and when I looked up at him, I got self-conscious.

"What's wrong?" he asked and stroked my cheek with his thumb.

"I'm not as good as all the puck bun—"

"Baby girl, that doesn't matter to me. If you don't want to do this, that's okay."

"But I want to."

He caressed my bottom lip. "Then show me how much with this pretty little mouth."

Heat coursed through me at his demanding words. I had some doubts I could be as good as the other women he had in his bed, but the way his eyes drank me in hungrily gave me the confidence to finish what I started.

I bent my head back down and licked him from root to tip. I held his cock with one hand and darted my tongue out to lick around the head. TJ fisted my hair, and I looked up at him with a grin. Seeing his head tipped back in pleasure turned me on. It made the anxiety of not being as good as the other women disappear.

I slid his cock between my lips, doing my best to take him as far as I could while pumping with my hand at the same time. I paused a couple of times to pop him out of my mouth. I caught my breath while I kissed and licked down his shaft, and then I slid his cock back inside my mouth.

He lifted my chin and pulled me off him. His thumb rubbed against the moisture on my cheek. "Your eyes are watering. I don't want to hurt you."

"S'okay," I slurred in pleasure. "More?" I kissed his thighs and stroked him with my hand.

"Nah. Get up here. I need to be inside of you."

"But—"

"Now, Maxine," he growled.

I stared at him for a second. I should have felt ashamed that his demanding nature turned me on, but I didn't. I liked how he was bossing me around in bed. I didn't feel awkward about sex when his hazel eyes drank me in like I was the only woman in his entire universe.

"Bed now," he growled again.

I jumped at the aggressiveness in his voice, but then I

climbed into the bed and laid back on it. I gestured to the boots on my feet. "Do I really need to leave my boots on?"

He laughed and stretched out on the bed beside me. He kissed me softly like he was trying to warm me up. But I didn't need it. Going down on him and seeing the look of ecstasy on his face was all I needed. I was soaked with my desire for him. That never happened to me before, but it was like TJ had unlocked my sexual desire.

"Indulge me, please," he said. He gave me that naughty grin again, and I caved.

I kissed him again, my fingers twirling into his hair, and not once did I feel guilty.

CHAPTER FIFTEEN

TJ

"You okay?" I asked her.

She looked up at me with lust-filled eyes. "TJ, please, I need you."

I trailed kisses down her body until I stopped at the valley of her breasts. I hefted one of them into my hand and flicked my tongue across her nipple. She moaned and wound her hand in my hair while I sucked and licked at her. I stroked her with my tongue until her nipple was a stark point. Then I repeated the action with her other breast until she was writhing beneath me and aching for release. Only then did I kiss my way down the rest of her body.

I parted her thighs and muscled my big body between them. I slid one finger across her slit and bit back a moan at how wet and ready she was. I looked up at her. "Oh, Max. Did sucking my dick turn you on?"

She nodded. "Uh-huh. TJ, I want you inside me right now, please."

I shook my head and grinned while I dipped my head

down and parted her with my tongue. I closed my eyes as I explored her, pressing her firmly into the mattress as I feasted on her sweet pussy. She tasted so good, and I wanted to taste her cum on my tongue again. I slid two thick fingers inside her tight entrance and applied more pressure when she arched her back and cried out.

"Oh, TJ, please," she moaned.

Whoa, I didn't hear those moans the first time we were together. I heard it when I went down on her, but hearing her beg for it was so fucking hot.

I lifted my head. "You want it bad, baby?"

She nodded.

"Too bad I'm not done eating yet."

"What?"

Instead of answering, I dipped my head back down and sucked her clit into my mouth. I moaned as I tasted her and worked her over with my fingers.

"Please, baby," she begged. "I want you right now!"

"Come for me first," I ordered.

I looked up at her, and she nodded vigorously. I curled my fingers up, searching for the secret spot deep inside of her. I knew I found it when she arched her back again and cried out my name. It was so sexy watching as the wave of her orgasm crashed over her. I'd give anything to watch her come like that again and again. I'd make it my job to make sure she never wanted for release ever again. Not when she was with me. Baby girl never had to ask for what she wanted. And with the taste of her still on my tongue, I knew exactly what she needed.

I untangled her legs from my shoulders and got out of the bed to get a condom. I sheathed my dick and got back into the bed, kneed her legs apart, and situated myself in-between them.

"You sure you want this?" I asked.

"Oh my God, please," she begged.

"You tell me if it's not working for you, okay?" I asked.

"You feel terrible you didn't make me come last time, don't you?"

"I felt like a dick. Like I ruined everything," I admitted.

She leaned up and cupped my face. "You didn't ruin anything. You're good at going down on me, so you've more than made up for it. Now please shut up and get inside me."

I laughed. "I love that you let your dirty side out with me."

"You make me feel okay with it. I feel safe with you, Tristan."

Only my sister and my parents called me Tristan, but I liked hearing my real name on her lips. I didn't think she realized it slipped out, though. More than anything, I wanted to hear her moan it while she came all over my dick.

I rubbed the head of my dick against her clit but didn't press inside her quite yet. She writhed beneath me, urging me to press on.

"Please, Tristan. I need you," she begged.

I gave her my lopsided grin. "You got me, baby girl."

I entered her slowly, teasing her with inch-by-delicious-inch of my dick. She wrapped her legs around my waist and dug the heels of her boots into my back. I rolled my hips in a slow rhythm and moved inside her. She felt so good that I had to remind myself not to come too quickly.

"Are you gonna come for me again?" I asked.

She bit her lip, and a tiny blush colored her cheeks. "Can you touch my clit?"

I pressed my thumb against her clit. "Good?"

"Yessss," she moaned.

"You just have to ask, and I'll give you what you want. I'll give you anything you want."

"It's hard for me."

I pressed deeper inside her, grinding my dick down into her so she felt every last inch. I gave her a cocky grin. "No, *this* is hard for you."

That broke the tension, and she rolled her eyes. But we both knew she secretly loved my ridiculousness.

I caressed her clit and thrust inside her, deep and slow. She closed her eyes and met my downward strokes with the arching of her hips. She felt like heaven, and I didn't want to stop. Her hand tangled in my hair as we kissed again, like we couldn't get enough of each other. I wanted to take her harder and faster, to make her cry out my name like I was the only man she'd ever come for.

My hand flew across her clit, and I drove into her hard. "Come for me, baby girl."

All she could do was nod in response, but she wrapped her legs around me tighter. I watched my dick sliding in and out of her pussy as I fucked her into ecstasy again. Until she squeezed her eyes shut and dug her nails into my shoulders.

"Tristan," she moaned. "Take me, hard. Take me like the bad man you are. Until I forget how to breathe."

Fuck me.

For a woman who said she didn't know how to ask for what she wanted, she certainly was asking for everything I ever wanted to give her.

I gave in to her desires until she came apart at the seams and was crying out my name. Then I was right behind her, slamming into her as hard as I could until I came in long, hot spurts.

I groaned out in relief and tried to catch my breath. She was doing the same, her chest heaving and her skin flushed.

Her lips were swollen from too many kisses, but I wanted to give her more.

"Good girl," I said to her.

A blush crossed her face, but she pulled me down for another passion-filled kiss. Not the kind you'd give to someone when you were embarrassed. This Max was the one I wanted to see more of. This Max came out of her shell and told me what she wanted. This was the secret dirty girl I knew she could be.

When we came up for air again, I finally pulled out of her and got up to get rid of the condom.

"Can I take my boots off now?" she asked with a grin and shook out a boot-clad leg.

I gave her my lopsided grin. "Yeah, I'll allow it."

She got out of bed and yanked her boots off before walking into the bathroom. She changed into a t-shirt to sleep in and returned to the bed. I slipped my boxers back on and laid down on the bed. I pulled her to my chest and cuddled her in my arms.

"Wow," she said and let out a breath.

"That good, eh?" I teased, then kissed the top of her head.

She twisted around so she could glare up at me. "Don't get cocky."

"Too late!"

"T?"

"Yeah?"

"Do you want to spend the night?" she asked and gave me a nervous look. I wasn't sure why she was nervous. This timid woman put a spell on me, and I had no desire to leave. Not tonight.

"I thought I already was."

She leaned up and kissed me. "Okay, well, I definitely

want you to."

We fell asleep with her wrapped up in my arms, and I knew I was in trouble when it came to her. I was letting my guard down because I really liked her and because I was tired of being lonely.

Holding her in my arms made me feel a little less alone. I wanted to try having a girlfriend, even with a woman as guarded as Maxine Monroe. I wanted to peel back the layers and discover all her secrets. I hadn't felt this way since high school, but Maxine wasn't Natalie. She wouldn't toy with my heart and cast me aside.

❄

I woke to a cry and then a blood-curdling scream. I shot up in bed in a daze when I realized I wasn't in my bed. I opened my eyes and blinked until I saw Maxine whimpering and crying in her sleep next to me.

I leaned over and tried to wake her. "Max, come on, baby. It's just a dream."

She shook her head, still asleep but crying. "No, no, there's so much blood. No, Charlie!"

Who's Charlie?

I pulled the tiny woman into my arms, cradling her in my lap. "Baby, wake up. You're having a nightmare."

She screamed again, and then footsteps pounded up the steps, and the door of her bedroom flung open. A tall Black woman in scrubs and long tiny braids in her hair stood staring at me.

"Shit," she swore.

Max was still whimpering but now into the crook of my neck and holding onto me in a death grip. I smoothed down her hair. "Hey, hey, wake up. Baby girl, I'm here. I've got you."

Her eyes fluttered open. "TJ?"

"Yeah, baby. You were having a nightmare."

She shook her head, and her eyes shifted to the woman standing at the foot of the bed. Then she was crying into my shoulder, and I held her close, not understanding what was happening.

"I'll go make some tea," the other woman said and left the room.

Max blubbered into my neck, and it broke my heart to see her shattered like this. I didn't understand what was happening or why she was crying in my arms. I just wanted to make her tears go away.

"Hey, what's going on?" I asked.

She shook her head.

"Max, tell me."

"No. Get to practice."

I glanced at my phone on the bedside table. I did need to get to practice, but making sure Max was okay was more important. I think I understood why Noah missed that practice when Dinah had the miscarriage that almost killed her. Some things were more important than hockey.

I couldn't believe I'd even thought that. Something about this timid woman brought down all my defenses and made me release the mask I wore all the time.

But she slipped out of my arms. "Just go, TJ."

"Max—"

"GO!" she snapped.

Seeing her tear-stained face as she told me to leave gutted me. I dressed and leaned over to kiss her goodbye.

"Hey, will you call me later?" I asked.

"Please, go. I don't want to talk about it right now."

Defeated, I walked down the steps but ran into her roommate in the kitchen. The woman gave me a sad smile. "So you're TJ Desjardins. Shorter than I thought."

I gave her a fake smile. "Skates make me look taller. You must be Keiana."

She stirred something into a steaming mug of liquid. "It's not your fault."

"What?"

She pointed upstairs. "Max has been through a lot. Just give her some space."

I ran a hand through my hair. "She told me about her parents. Is that what this is?"

She eyed me carefully. "In a way, yes. What has she told you?"

"That a drunk driver killed her parents."

She sighed. "She didn't tell you the full story. Max is fragile. If you're the type of guy who flinches at anxiety or women who cry for no reason, you need to cut her loose now. Don't let her get attached to you if you're gonna run at the first sight of issues."

I stared at her. "I haven't had a girlfriend since high school, and she messed me up pretty bad. I don't want to mess up with Max."

She pointed at me. "Right answer! Okay, hockey boy, get to practice."

"Hockey boy? That's what she calls me."

Keiana laughed. "I know—it was my idea. By the way... she secretly loves that you call her baby girl, but don't tell her I said anything to you."

I grinned. "Ha! Knew it!"

She mimed zipping her lips. "Give her some space, TJ, but she'll come around."

I nodded in response and then left, so I wasn't late for practice.

My head was a mess, though, and I ended up having the shittest performance ever on the ice. Something was wrong with my girl, and instead of leaning on me for support, she pushed me away. And that made the doubt climb inside my head again.

I stripped off my jersey, annoyed and frustrated with how shitty I had been at practice.

"Bud, you okay?" Noah asked me for the fifty-millionth time afterward.

"Fuck, no!"

"You want to talk about it?" he asked.

"No. It's fine."

He raised his eyebrows at me, but I didn't say anything else before we left to carpool back to the city.

When I got home, my sister knew something was up. I knew someone had snitched on me if she was here.

"Hey, what's wrong?" she asked.

Benny and her shared a look, and she dragged me down onto the couch with her. Benny took the seat next to her and gave her a quick kiss before letting her return her attention to me.

I put my head in my hands. "I don't know."

"What happened?"

"Maxine woke up screaming this morning and then kicked me out. I've never seen her like that before, and I..."

"You wanted to be there for her, but she pushed you away."

I nodded.

Rox put a hand on my shoulder. "Maybe give her some space? This isn't about you."

"Rox, it was so scary seeing her like that."

"It'll be okay, Tristan. You need to give her a bit of time. How was everything before that?"

I smiled. "Fantastic. I don't know what happened."

Benny stroked his beard. "Sometimes, dude, you have to be patient with women. Even if they're frustrating creatures that don't tell you what they want."

My sister flicked him the bird, and he laughed and pulled her hand to his chest. "Like this one. Did you ever think I'd tame your sister?"

"Okay, buddy, you didn't tame Roxie. She pulls you around by the dick."

"HA!" my sister laughed. "He likes it."

Benny kissed her temple and shrugged. "Best thing to ever happen to me."

I sighed. "Ugh, you two are gross."

But the thing was, I was jealous of my sister and Benny. Especially now that my girl kicked me out of her house this morning. I wanted to hold her and dry her tears, but she wouldn't let me.

Was I destined to never find happiness? Maybe all the cruel things Nat said to me in high school were true. I was just a stupid jock who was easily replaceable. I should have been content with fucking my way through all of Philadelphia with women who didn't care about me. But Maxine had put me under her spell, and I didn't want things to end here.

CHAPTER SIXTEEN

MAXINE

I laid on my bed and stared at the text message chain with TJ. Instead of getting ready for work, I was still lying in bed. I was taking a mental health day for sure. I had already texted Rox to tell her I needed one, but she hadn't responded yet.

I'd felt like the biggest jerk in the world since I kicked TJ out of my house this past weekend. Especially after an amazing night of incredible sex where I didn't feel guilty or shameful at all. Then I had another dream about the accident and woke up crying in TJ's arms. I didn't want him to see what he'd deal with if he was with me.

I hadn't heard from him since that night, and I worried he'd realized what a mess I was. There was a reason I didn't open myself up to people. Why I haven't had a relationship since Charlie. I didn't deserve it, and the other person didn't deserve to have to suffer over my mental health issues.

My heartbeat was too loud in my head. I dropped my phone and tried to focus on my breathing. My breath came in jagged pants...and that's how I knew I was having a panic attack.

I hated this. I hated feeling this way. Like I was going to jump out of my skin. My thoughts were too loud, pounding into me as I freaked out about the state of my life.

My phone buzzed on my bed. I grabbed it and pressed it to my ear with a shaky hand as I tried to control my breathing. My hands were sweaty, and I felt like it was getting harder to breathe.

"Max, are you there?" Rox asked.

"Y-yy-yes," I stammered back at her.

"Oh, Maxine. Are you having a panic attack? Are you okay?"

I never wanted to tell Rox what happened to me, but when I had a panic attack over a big meeting with Quinn, Rox's boss, she pulled me into her office and made me tell her everything. Roxanne Desjardins was a loud-mouth, feisty woman, but she also fought for the people she loved. When she let me blubber on her shoulder, I knew I could trust her.

"No, I'm not fucking okay," I finally admitted in a small voice.

Rox was silent for a moment. "I don't think I've ever heard you say 'fuck' before."

I ran a hand down my face, still feeling the effects of my anxiety-induced panic attack, but talking with Rox was helping. "It comes out sometimes. I save those for a rainy day."

"Okay, so safe to say you need this mental health day?"

"Yes. I'm sorry."

"Don't apologize. Listen, have you talked to my brother?"

"No."

"I told him to give you space."

Oh.

That's why he hadn't contacted me. I didn't want space. I wanted TJ to be here with me, and I wanted to feel his arms around me and hear him call me his 'baby girl.' But I had messed everything up by letting my fears about my late boyfriend and my trauma invade my life.

"I pushed him away," I said.

"I know, but it's gonna be okay."

"He's not even my boyfriend. We've only gone on a couple dates."

She sighed. "Oh my God, he so is and you know it! Call my brother already and make him come over there and cuddle you, okay? He's been mopey since you kicked him out and playing like shit."

"What?"

"Call my brother!"

Then she hung up on me.

I stared back at my phone as the call disconnected. Then I pulled up the text chain with TJ again. I typed and deleted and then typed and deleted until I got out one word.

ME: *Hi.*

He wrote back seconds later.

TJ: *Hey, baby girl.*

I bit my lip. I heard his voice in my head calling me that and giving me his sexy, lopsided grin. I loved his naughty smile, like he was always up to no good. Which he usually was. TJ was loud and in your face while I was meek like a mouse. We were complete opposites, but I loved that about us.

ME: *I'm sorry about the other night.*

TJ: *It's okay.*

ME: *It's not!*

TJ: *No...but I was worried about you. Still am.*

ME: *Can you come over? I need to see you.*

TJ: *I have practice but then I can come. Don't you have work?*

ME: *No, I'm taking a sick day. I...I just can't today.*

TJ: *Okay. I'll see you soon.*

I dropped my phone onto my bedside table and pulled the blankets up on my chest. I had no desire to get out of bed or get dressed. Even if TJ was going to see me later. I really needed this mental health day. I slipped into sleep after a weekend of tossing and turning.

I stirred at the sound of footsteps on the stairs, but I ignored it because I thought it was Keiana. I didn't even open my eyes. Not when my bedroom door creaked open or when I felt a weight dip down in my bed. I curled into the bed and the warmth it provided.

My alarm went off what felt like seconds later and a groan sounded from behind me. Startled, I reached for my phone but realized there was a large forearm wrapped around my waist and a big thigh entangled with mine. A warm, muscular chest was pressed up against my back. I shut off my alarm and shifted onto my back to find TJ half-asleep beside me.

Did he seriously come over and nap with me? That was...kind of sweet.

Hazel eyes popped open and stared down at me. I could get lost in those storms of greens and browns. He leaned over me and reached a hand up to brush my hair behind my ear. That cute, lopsided grin etched across his face.

"Hi," I whispered.

"Hey, yourself," he whispered back, then pressed a gentle kiss on my forehead.

"How long have you been here?" I asked through a yawn.

He checked his phone. "An hour. Keiana let me in. You were half-asleep, and it seemed like you needed it. Roxie told me you had a panic attack earlier and you needed cuddles."

I laughed. "You and your sister are a bit too close."

"I know! Benny always says it's like dating both of us. But she's my best friend, and we tell each other everything."

My eyes bugged out of my head. "Everything?"

He laughed. "Um...not all the details. I would never tell her anything that makes you uncomfortable."

"Did you tell her about..."

He frowned. "That you faked it the first time?"

I grimaced.

He stroked my cheek. "It's okay, baby. I just wanted her advice. I thought I did something wrong."

"It probably wasn't your fault. I think it was my complicated feelings about sex."

"But since then it's been okay, right?"

He seemed nervous, like our time together hadn't been good enough for me. But TJ was attentive to my needs and asked what I wanted. He hadn't done that the first time we slept together, but since then, he took the extra effort to make sure I felt good. I had never expected him to be such a considerate lover.

I nodded and snuggled down into his chest, laying my head against his heart. He had stripped down to his boxers, but he felt so warm, and he smelled of clean laundry and manly ocean-scented soap. He smelled like home and comfort, and I sighed in contentment at him stroking my hair. The thump-thump-thump of his heart was a calming noise in my ear.

"I'm sorry," I said into his chest.

He kissed the top of my head. "We don't have to talk about it if you don't want to."

"TJ, I haven't had a boyfriend since high school for a reason. You don't want to be with a fragile, broken woman who has panic attacks."

He tilted my chin up to look at him. "What makes you think I'm not in it for the long haul?"

"Because you're you!"

He furrowed his brow, and I knew I'd hit a nerve. "What the fuck does that mean?"

I pulled away from him and sat up against my headboard. "TJ, you have a reputation as quite the ladies' man. You don't do relationships. Why would you be interested in me anyway? You can have anyone you want—you usually do."

He sat against the headboard with me. "I hate that you say things like that about yourself. I like you, Max, I really do. I've been dumb about women, too afraid of getting hurt that I didn't put myself out there. Last year, I dated this girl, but I insisted I wanted something casual. I didn't realize it was a mistake until she was gone. Then I met you when I was visiting my sister at work."

"To be fair, we'd met before," I pointed out.

"I know. Noah reminded me of that, but I never talked to you. I was half expecting you to not give me your number, but then you did, and I was too chicken-shit to ask you out."

I raised an eyebrow at him. "So, wait, the reason you never called wasn't because you moved on to the next puck bunny? It was because you were afraid?"

He nodded sheepishly. "Yeah, but I couldn't stop thinking about you. Then I felt bad about that first night. I thought I had messed everything up, but then you gave me a second chance. When you kicked me out, it felt like I fucked up again."

My face fell, and I had to blink back tears. I never wanted him to feel like it was his fault.

He reached a hand out to brush aside the tears. "Aw, baby girl. Why are you crying?"

"I'm sorry I pushed you away. It's hard for me to get close to people."

He sighed and ran a hand through his hair. "Believe me, I understand that. We're quite the pair, eh?"

I laughed.

He pulled me into his lap until I was straddling his thighs. I pressed my forehead against his, and his hands traveled down my back to rest on my hips. He leaned up and captured my lips with his. He kissed me tentatively, exploring my mouth like he had all the time in the world. I wound my hands into his thick, dark hair as I parted my lips. I moaned when his tongue slipped inside, exploring my depths.

I pulled back and smiled at him. "Did you really come over just to give me cuddles and make me feel better?"

He grinned up at me, shooting me that cocky grin I loved, but I knew behind it was a man who was afraid to let his feelings show. "Maybe. Men can like cuddling too, you know! I wanted to know you were okay."

I nodded. "I am, now that you're here." I ground against him, feeling his hard length growing underneath me. "I feel like I need to make it up to you."

"The only way you need to make it up to me is by telling me you're officially my girl."

I grinned. "Okay...yeah."

"Yeah?" he asked, and his eyes lit up as he smiled at me.

I cupped his firm jaw in my delicate hands. "Yeah. Because you're my man."

"I like the sound of that. I want to be your boyfriend... but I'm afraid I'm not gonna be good enough at it."

"I'm afraid I'm not the girlfriend you want," I admitted.

"I guess we'll figure it out together."

I kissed him again and thought about how happy he made me. I pulled back and peeled my t-shirt off, revealing my naked chest.

"Fuck yeah, no bra!" he cheered as he reached two meaty hands up to cup my breasts while I kissed his neck.

I laughed.

"Bras suck, baby. They're booby prisons."

"TJ, you're too much sometimes."

He gave me that lopsided grin again while he played with my nipples, and I ground against his lap. His hands felt *so* good on me.

"Please keep touching me," I moaned.

One hand stayed where it was, but the other slid down my torso and into my *super* sexy cotton panties. Had I known he was coming over, I might have changed into something sexier. TJ didn't seem to mind; he cared more about getting inside them than what they looked like.

He had that sexy grin on his face again when his finger found my clit. "Is that all for me, baby girl?"

I grinned and kissed him again, hungrily sucking on his tongue while he pressed two thick fingers inside me. I shamelessly rocked my hips against his hand.

It had only been a couple of days without him, but I missed him. He made me feel safe to give into my desires, and I didn't feel shame when I was with him. I let go of my fears, and pressed myself further against his hand, getting mine and for once not thinking too hard about it.

"Right there, yes," I moaned. "TJ, I need you right now."

He grinned at me. "Yeah? Do you want to ride my cock?"

I paused. "Um…I've never done that before."

He took his fingers out of me and I pouted, but then he gingerly laid me down on the bed. He spread my thighs and slid my underwear down my legs.

"Maxine, have you ever had sex that wasn't missionary?" he asked.

I shook my head.

"What? Seriously? Okay, let's find out what positions you like."

"Wait, what?"

He grinned at me. "There's more than just the missionary position, you know. Let's figure out what you like the best, okay?"

He got off of the bed, slipped his boxers down his legs and rolled a condom on. He walked over to my bedside table and found the lube. He slicked it down his sheathed cock, and he got back into the bed.

He crooked a finger at me. "C'mere and hop on my dick."

My face flushed, but the hungry look he gave me made me straddle his hips. He helped me by taking my hand in his so I could grab hold of him, and he helped me guide his cock to my entrance. I slid down onto him, and I loved the feeling of being able to set the pace.

"I don't know what I'm doing, T," I admitted shyly.

His hands roamed down and held onto my hips. He thrusted up into me, and I sighed at the feeling of him hard and needy inside of me. "Relax and do what feels good. Ride my dick and let me touch those titties."

I laughed. He was lucky he was so cute, or I'd be annoyed with that comment. I couldn't help the grin that spread across my face when he gave me that naughty smile as he dipped his head down and put one of my breasts in his mouth.

I slid up and down on his cock, setting the pace nice and slow. I gasped when he pressed his thumb against my clit.

He lifted his head up from my chest. "That feel good?"

I nodded as I pressed my hands on his chest and rode him faster. "Uh-huh."

"Love watching my dick sliding in and out of your pretty pussy," he growled.

"Oh...I kinda like when you talk dirty to me."

He grinned. "Oh, yeah?"

I nodded. "I think you're helping me be okay with my sexuality."

"Hell yes! I'm gonna help you let your freak flag fly," he cheered.

He played with my clit until I couldn't take it anymore, and I was riding him hard and moaning his name.

"Come for me. That's a good girl," he growled. He gripped my hips in both of his hands, pulling me further down on him.

Hmm, I liked him calling me a good girl.

A lot.

Who knew I was into that? Not me, that was for sure.

TJ was so open to finding what worked for me, and that turned me on. For a guy known as a playboy, it surprised me he cared so much about his partner's needs.

"Be a good girl and come all over my cock," he ordered.

I whimpered and nodded.

He thrusted up inside of me hard and fast, and then I tumbled down inside myself as he brought me to the brink again. I screamed out his name while he pressed his cock inside me faster and faster while I came. Then he groaned beneath me, and I felt the final pulsing of his orgasm inside me.

I tried to catch my breath and gave him a smile. We were both sweaty, and our chests were heaving from the exertion. But I didn't feel shame or dirty from the sex. Instead, I wanted to do it again. TJ nuzzled my breasts and kissed one, then the other, which made me laugh. I disentangled myself from him and went to the bathroom to clean myself up. When I came back to bed, TJ was lying on his back with his eyes closed. He looked so relaxed, and I loved that I did that.

His eyes popped open when I crawled back into bed, and he pulled me back onto his chest. "Are you hungry?" he asked.

I laughed and looked at the clock. It was one in the afternoon, and I hadn't eaten since I had a protein bar this morning when I was attempting to go to work. "Yes, I'm starving. Let's get something to eat."

CHAPTER SEVENTEEN

TJ

My girl was all smiles as she sat next to me at her kitchen table, shoveling a veggie burger into her face. I was shirtless because she had commandeered my t-shirt, and it fell to her mid-thighs like a dress. She had her legs stretched out on my lap, and I was absentmindedly running my hand up one of them while I ate my burger. She had worked up an appetite after all the sex we had upstairs, and it was cute watching her shovel down food like a hockey player.

"You better stop rubbing my leg," she warned.

I grinned. "Oh, yeah?"

"Yeah, because I'm probably gonna pounce on you again."

I barked out a laugh. "Did I unlock something in you today?"

She blushed, a sign of her uncertainty with sex. It was cute, but I saw how she looked when she was riding my dick earlier. Her lush lips had parted and her eyes closed in ecstasy as she took what she needed from me.

And Maxine liked dirty talk. That was a revelation I hadn't expected. It was fucking hot. I wondered how long it would take me to convince her to try doggy-style.

I wanted to help her find out what she liked, to help her feel comfortable in the bedroom. This thing between us wasn't just sex for me. I came to her house because my sister told me Max was having a hard time. That wasn't something I've ever done with a hookup before. Rox's words had been, 'Go cuddle your girlfriend and make her feel better.' To which I said, 'She's not my girlfriend,' but my sister hung up on me instead. She'd be smug when I told her it was official.

I haven't had a girlfriend since Natalie, and that was terrible. Nat was the reason I walled myself off and had casual hookup after casual hookup. It took Taylor leaving to figure that out. Max was shy and had some demons to battle, but she wouldn't play games with my heart. When I held her in my arms today and breathed in the floral scent of her body wash, I knew I wanted more. Laying in bed with her made me feel like I was home.

Max poked me with her foot. "What are you thinking about?"

I smiled and stole one of her fries.

"Hey! I was eating that!" she protested.

"Too slow," I said with a smirk, and finished my bite. I didn't think Max understood yet how much hockey players needed to eat.

She smiled at me as I 'helped' her finish the rest of her fries. She then removed her feet from my lap and cleared the plates off the table. She tossed everything in the garbage, but when she came to sit back down, I grabbed her around the waist and pulled her into my lap, forcing her to straddle me.

I threaded my hands into her hair, and she wrapped hers around the back of my neck. I was already hard, and she probably felt it, since my dick was pressing against the zipper of my jeans, begging to be inside her again. She kissed me tentatively at first, and I let her set the pace until our tongues were tangling again and our hands were roaming. We would have fucked right there if the sound of someone clearing their throat didn't pull us away.

Max's pale face was red in embarrassment, but I smirked. It wasn't the first time I'd been caught in a compromising position. But for Max, this sort of stuff was difficult, so I pressed a reassuring kiss to her temple before glancing at her roommate, Keiana.

Keiana wasn't in scrubs like the last time I saw her. She was wearing a pair of jeans and a t-shirt, but she looked tired. She slammed down a comically large box of condoms on the kitchen table. "Here, you two need this. But don't fuck in my kitchen!"

Max buried her head in the crook of my neck and repositioned herself so she was sitting on my lap as opposed to straddling me like she was about to mount me. Keiana and I shared a conspiratorial look and laughed. Max buried her head further into my neck, which wasn't helping my downstairs situation.

Max finally lifted her head from my neck. "There's a burger in the fridge for you," she said to her roommate.

Keiana walked over to the fridge. "Okay, you're forgiven. But also, go you! I think I like you, hockey boy!"

"Me? Why?" I asked.

Keiana dug a plate out of the cabinet and heated her food up in the microwave. "Because you make Max break out of her shell a little. Don't get me wrong, I didn't want to have to hear it, but she's heard her fair share of banging headboards from my room."

I kissed Max's forehead and held her tighter. "Could be worse. Could come home and hear your sister and your roommate fucking loudly," I said with a shudder.

Max pulled back to look at me with her mouth hanging open. "Wait, is that how you found out about Rox and Benny?"

I nodded with a grimace. "Don't remind me."

Keiana laughed. "You brought it up, dude." She walked over to the table and sat down across from us. She smirked at Max, but then shook her head.

"Don't give me that," Max said.

"Just happy for you. Hey, hockey boy, have you two made this official yet?"

I nodded. "Yeah, she finally agreed to be my girl."

The dark-skinned woman beamed at me. "Good...but you know women can get blood out of everything. I'm a nurse. I know things."

It was cute how all the women in Max's life threatened my life if I broke her heart. Like my sister, who threatened to break my hand or cut me with her skate blade if I broke Max's heart. My sister threw around this 'I don't give a fuck about you' attitude, but she cared about the people around her, and she had a soft spot for Max.

"Well, my twin sister basically threatened my hockey career, so I got the message already," I said.

"She did?" Max asked. Her face contorted into a confused look.

I nodded and pushed her hair out of her face. "If my sister likes you, that's always good news."

Max beamed at me and got off of my lap. She grabbed

the box of condoms. "Come on, hockey boy. Let's go make use of these."

Keiana's mouth flopped open at Max's words, and my girl gave her a sly smile. I wasn't sure what it was about me that brought down her defenses, I loved that I made her feel safe enough that she felt she could do that.

I followed my girlfriend upstairs to her room and let her experiment on me for the rest of the day. If a mental health day means having marathon sex with your partner to figure out their sexual desires, I think it should damn well be a national holiday.

❄

I woke to a whimper and Max clutching my arm. I hated seeing her like this.

I pried her fingers off me and pulled her to my chest, tucking my chin on top of her head. "Shush, baby girl, it's okay," I tried to soothe her. I rubbed my hands up and down her back. I heard her sniffling and felt the salty tears sliding down my chest. "Aw, hell, Maxine. Wake up, baby."

Her head tilted up to me, tears in her eyes, and it broke me. I held her tighter to my chest. "TJ?" she asked. "Why are you squeezing me so hard?"

"You were crying in your sleep again."

She pulled away and sat up on the bed, hugging her knees to her chest. "I'm sorry."

I sat up too but shook my head. "Don't be sorry. You want to talk about it?"

She shook her head, but she wasn't looking at me. Instead, she stared blankly at a spot on the wall.

"Max, is it like this every night?"

"No. Only when I'm feeling happy," she admitted.

"What do you mean?"

She picked at her nail and still wouldn't look at me. "Because I don't deserve to be happy."

"Of course, you deserve happiness."

She shook her head, tears falling down her face, and I didn't know what I should do to help her.

"No, I shouldn't be alive. I—" She cut herself off with another cry.

My heart wrenched in my chest at her words. I pulled her into me again, and this time, she didn't pull away. "Tell me about it?" I asked.

"I was in the car," she said in a small voice.

Oh.

"When your parents died? You survived?"

She pointed to the scar above her eyebrow that I always wondered about but never asked about. "I was the only survivor."

I leaned down to kiss her eyebrow. "I'm so sorry. I can't imagine what you went through."

"TJ, I need to be honest with you about why I'm awkward about sex and why I get panic attacks. If you really want to be my boyfriend, you have to understand how damaged I am."

"Max," I started to say, but she held up a hand to stop me. I clamped my mouth shut and let her speak.

"I told you my parents were super religious. I had sex with my boyfriend in high school, and they found out."

"How?"

She sighed. "Mom went fishing in my trashcan. I didn't think she would! She berated me about pre-marital sex being wrong for hours and told me that God would punish me for my sins."

I wasn't religious. Mom made us go to church for

Christmas and Easter, but I didn't have a strict upbringing like Max. I couldn't imagine what that was like.

"We were driving home from graduation..." She choked off into a sob, and I reached out to squeeze her hand. "Charlie was with us. All of them died, except for me. I shouldn't have survived when they didn't."

Charlie was the name she called out when she was still asleep. It all made sense to me now.

I wanted to wrap her around in my arms and never let her go. I wanted to keep her safe forever and make sure nothing bad ever happened to her again. I'd wrap her up in bubble wrap if I had to.

I lifted her hand to my mouth and kissed the back of her palm. "Maxine, you weren't the drunk driver. You didn't cause this. It sucks you went through that traumatic experience, but you deserve all the happiness you can get, and I want to give it to you."

She wiped her eyes and didn't let go of my hand. "Why? Before you met me, you only hit it and quit it. You said there was someone else before me, and you messed up with her. Am I her replacement?"

I shook my head vigorously.

Maxine wasn't Taylor. When I was with Taylor, I knew it wasn't permanent. Hell, I never even called her my girl. I was an asshole to her. I didn't sleep with other women, but I definitely thought about it. I didn't have those same feelings with Max. Something about Max made me want to throw away my playboy lifestyle. She made me believe I could have those things I longed for but thought I didn't deserve.

"Do you want to know why I haven't had anything serious with anyone since high school?" I asked.

She nodded and curled herself into my arms.

"In high school, I dated this girl Natalie. She was hot."

Her laughter interrupted me. "Ohhh, shocker!"

"Quiet, you," I teased and kissed her temple. "Well, anyway... She was the hottest girl in school, and I was the star hockey player. But she played games. She'd cheat on me, then we'd get back together, and then the cycle would repeat itself. She expected me to know exactly what she wanted without telling me. She kissed my sister on a dare at a party, and that was the last straw."

"Why?"

"I've never had a problem with Roxie being bisexual, and it didn't surprise me when she came out," I explained. "Natalie did it to get a rise out of me, though. She was always doing stuff like that. She was always insulting me too, telling me I was just another dumb jock and she could find another one."

Max shifted in my lap so she was straddling me. Her hands cupped my jaw. "Oh, baby. I'm so sorry."

I leaned into her touch. "She made me feel like I wasn't worthy of love, that I didn't deserve it. When I got drafted, it was over between us, and I never opened myself up to anyone else."

"Until now."

He nodded. "Nat's apologized since, and Rox's still friends with her. Nat's changed a lot. I even like her husband! But the hurt's still there."

Max's hand trailed down my chest, and she placed it over my heart. "It's still in here."

I nodded and placed my hand over hers. "I understand feeling like you're not worthy or that we don't deserve what we found with each other."

She kissed me but pulled away before I could glide my tongue across the seam of her lips. "I'm sorry you have to deal with my nightmares."

"I told you, I'm in it for the long haul with you. But..."

"But what?"

I squinted up at her, unsure if this would cause her to get pissed at me. "Have you talked with someone about how you feel?"

"Like a shrink?"

"Therapy's nothing to be ashamed of. You should talk to someone about your nightmares."

She bit her lip. "I'll think about it."

"I'm serious, Max."

Her lips drew into a thin line. "I said I'll think about it."

"Why are you so against it? I went to a sports psychologist."

"Really?" she asked with a hint of surprise in her voice.

I nodded. "It really helped me when I was a rookie. My dad...he was a hockey player too. He always wanted me to have the best training and that meant my mind, too."

She sighed. "It's just...my parents didn't believe in strangers knowing our business. That God would sort things out. They even scoffed that our church offered counseling. They thought it was beneath them."

"Do you believe that?" I asked. Max didn't strike me as being all that religious anymore, so I didn't understand why she was fighting this.

"No." she admitted. "But I don't want to talk about that night ever. It hurts too much."

"Max—"

"Geez. I said I'll think about it, okay?" she huffed out and got off my lap.

Great, now she was annoyed with me.

She flopped onto the bed and laid on her side with her back to me. I curled around her, hugging her petite frame against my chest. "Please, baby? I hate seeing you like this, and I don't know how to help you."

"Okay," she muttered meekly.

I frowned because I thought she said that so I'd stop pushing her. I wanted to take all her pain away, but I didn't know how. The only thing I could do was hold her closer and tell her everything was going to be okay.

CHAPTER EIGHTEEN

MAXINE

If there was one thing I learned about being TJ Desjardins' girlfriend over the past couple of months, it was that being a hockey WAG was weird. And challenging.

Sometimes I'd get a day or two of him being around, and then before I knew it, he was back on the road again. It felt like we were constantly stealing tiny moments together before he was rushing out to catch a bus or a team charter for another game. Sometimes, the first time I saw him again was from behind the glass at a home game.

Today was one of those days.

We didn't have time to catch each other before he had to get to the arena, so the first time I saw him again was when I watched him skating around the zone during warmups. And, of course, he didn't notice me because TJ got inside his head during games and tried to block out the crowd.

I wasn't sure I would have survived this life if I hadn't

formed strong friendships with the other girls. Especially with Rox.

"Is Fi gonna come?" Rox asked Dinah.

Dinah shook her head. "She's balls deep in edits right now. Riley understands."

I almost spit out my drink. Dinah and Rox always said what they were thinking, and it still came as a shock to me at times. They also had mouths worse than hockey players. TJ's words, not mine.

I kept my swearing to a minimum, but lately, it had been coming out more. Mostly during sex. If I was riding TJ, or underneath him, or he had me bent over the bed, swear words that used to make me blush flew out of my mouth. And I didn't care because being with TJ was like he unlocked the cage I had been trapped in.

Rox poked my arm. "What are you thinking about?"

"Sex," I blurted out and clamped a hand over my mouth.

While that was true, I didn't mean to say that out loud. I rubbed a hand over the back of my neck, but my face was flushed and hot at the admittance.

Dinah let out a loud laugh. And holy crap, that tiny girl had a booming laugh. She had such a big personality, which made sense since Noah was such a quiet, sensitive guy.

Rox blanched and pretended to put her finger down her throat. "Gross, I've already been scarred for life now."

I cringed and gave her a pained look.

Last night, we thought we had the condo to ourselves. I didn't realize Benny and Rox were there until TJ's phone kept vibrating with a text from his sister telling him I was being 'loud AF.' At the time, I had been lost in pleasure, but now I could barely look Rox in the eye.

Rox laughed. "Oh my god, you should see how red your

face is! For the record, I'm so happy for you. I haven't seen Tristan this happy in...well, I can't remember the last time."

"Can I ask you guys something weird?" I asked. I bit my nails and felt the blush creeping up my neck again.

Shut up, Max. Don't even ask them your weird, naïve question. What are you doing?

Rox raised a dark eyebrow, clearly intrigued, and I hoped I didn't gross her out by my question.

"It's a sex question," I said and stared down into my plastic cup of wine.

Dinah put a hand on my leg. "Honey, you don't need to be taught the birds and bees, right?"

"No! It's...not that...I...um..." I sputtered and put my hands over my face.

"Oh my God, spit it out!" Rox exclaimed and took a sip of her beer with the shake of her head.

I pulled my hands away from my face and turned to both of them. They looked giddy with anticipation. "Um...is it weird if a guy calls you a 'good girl' in bed?"

Dinah barked out a loud laugh and then chugged her beer. Rox stared at me open-mouthed.

Dinah finished her beer and laughed again. "Holy fuck. That was NOT what I thought you were going to ask. But no, I don't think it's weird...if you're into that thing, but everyone's different. Some dudes like to be called Daddy."

She made a face.

"Don't kink shame, D!" Rox teased.

Dinah held up her hands in surrender. "No judgment, it's just not my thing!"

I nodded in agreement. TJ asked for that once, but we both decided it wasn't for us. He preferred me moaning his name instead.

"I prefer the opposite," Rox said with a grin. "But if

you're both good with it, there's nothing weird about it. Yeah, I'm not a fan of the Daddy thing, but everyone has their tastes."

I stared blankly at Rox. "What do you mean, the opposite?"

Now Rox was the one with pink cheeks. "I like to be called a bad girl, okay?" she muttered under her breath.

"Oh...oh! Sorry I asked," I said.

I felt the blush color on my face at her revelation. I didn't need to know that. I shouldn't have asked her to clarify. Why did I ask her that?

"Noah calls me the Boss Lady if you were wondering," Dinah said with a cheeky grin. "I like to be in charge."

I was not, in fact, wondering, and I think I opened a can of worms by asking them this. That explained some things about Noah, though. On the ice, you didn't want to face-off with him, but off the ice, he seemed like the nicest guy on the team. And the way he doted on Dinah? So cute.

I drank more of my wine to avoid them asking more questions. Despite the chill in the arena, my face felt hot, and I couldn't look either of them in the eye. Especially not Rox.

Rox shook with laughter. "Sorry, Max. I know these things are hard to talk about for you."

I nodded. "TJ's been helping me with that. I know he's your brother, and you don't want to hear this, but being with him doesn't make me feel guilty or shameful."

Rox's face softened. "Aw, Max, I think you might love my brother."

My eyes were as wide as saucers. "I—"

"Christ, Roxanne, don't scare the girl," Dinah cut in. "Honey, I'm glad you got with T. I've watched him over the years have meaningless hookup after meaningless hookup, and when he was upset over Taylor last year, I think it was a wake-up call. TJ can be a little douchey, but he's a good guy."

I gave her a small smile. Dinah seemed like a good friend, and I was glad she was in TJ's corner.

The first period was getting underway, so I turned my attention back to the ice. My heart pounded in my chest when I saw TJ on the starting line-up, but I saw the team captain Girard taking the opening face-off.

I loved hockey. I loved the smell of the ice, the roar of the crowd, and the sounds of hockey sticks tapping against the ice. Being in this arena to watch my team, to watch my man duking it out with the Toronto Wolves, was amazing. TJ asked me before about my passion, and it was this sport. I might hate being in sales, but I loved working for the team.

I watched the play on the ice and laughed when Rox yelled at the refs about a blown call. Rox was loud and opinionated, and I loved her for it. I jumped in my seat when TJ carried the puck over the blue line, passed it to Noah, but then it went off the post. TJ scrambled to get the rebound, and I was screaming my head off for him to shoot, but then the Wolves' goalie covered it, issuing the stoppage of play.

"Bullshit," I said under my breath and took another sip of my wine.

Dinah and Rox both stared at me.

"What?" I asked.

Rox tipped back her head and laughed. "It's weird hearing you swear."

I shrugged but went back to watching the game. TJ was back on the bench, chewing on his mouth guard, but he was chirping at the opposing players. He was scrappy on the ice. He was the guy who got under the other player's skins. Bad for other teams, but awesome for the Bulldogs. A Wolves player skated by, and I noticed the name Holmstrom on the back of his jersey.

"Oh, that's Blaise," I said, recognizing my old high school classmate.

Dinah raised a questioning eyebrow. "You know Blaise Holmstrom?"

"We went to high school together. He used to cheat off of my tests in math class."

"Oh, right, TJ mentioned you went to Franklin Prep. Fancy."

I laughed. "Scholarship! I can't believe we're both from South Philly and didn't know each other."

Dinah laughed. "You want to hear something funny?"

"What?" I asked.

"My brother Eddie does all of Blaise's tattoos."

"Shut up!"

Dinah laughed, and Rox watched the players on the ice wistfully. "He's so hot. And he's bisexual!"

That had been a shock when Blaise came out last year. Especially since he had been dating the same girl since high school. If I hadn't met Rox and gotten an education on sexuality, that would have confused me.

I pinched Rox's side. "You're taken!"

"I know!" she said with a laugh. "But if I wasn't with Benny…"

I shook my head at her. "Blaise has a long-distance girlfriend back in Sweden."

"Sweden?" Rox asked with a grimace. "And I complain about not getting laid when Benny's gone for a week on the road."

I shrugged and watched the ice, but not much was happening. The Bulldogs hadn't been able to set anything up yet. Although the Wolves had a pretty good D out in front of them.

"Doesn't his dad own Eileen's?" Dinah asked.

I nodded. "Yeah, he co-owns it with one of his old teammates. One of his other sons is the manager there."

"I always feel safe there because Hal looks out for us," Rox said.

A small smile spread across my face. I knew exactly what she meant.

The conversation died down when the crowd got loud again. I brought my attention back to the ice and saw TJ was suddenly on the breakaway. Finally, the game was getting exciting.

I jumped up from my seat, nearly knocking my wine all over Rox as I cheered on my man. He had this! He deked around the Wolves' defenseman and took the shot. We all cheered when it went top shelf, and the red lamp lit up behind the goaltender.

"Eat a dick, Wolves!" Dinah yelled.

Rox busted up laughing. "Holy fuck, D, you savage!"

She shrugged with a cheeky grin, and Mia, Hallsy's girl, turned around in her seat in front of us. "Will you loud-mouths settle down?"

"But they're playing like garbage!" Rox protested.

I swatted her to settle her. "Come on, girl, watch your man on the ice."

She nudged me with her shoulder. "You watch your man."

I grinned at her. "Oh, I will."

Mia laughed again. "I never thought TJ, of all the guys, would finally settle down. Good for you, Max. He needs a good girl like you to keep him in check."

Dinah was trying so hard not to laugh. The wink Mia gave me told me she had been listening to our conversation. I should have been mortified. I should have wanted to melt into a puddle under my seat. But I didn't want to do any of that. Because being with TJ made me forget about my guilt. He made me feel free.

CHAPTER NINETEEN

TJ

"So, you and the cute blonde?" Logan nudged me while I fixed my tie in my cubby and combed my hair with my fingers.

"Who? Max? Yeah, that's my girl."

The redheaded d-man smirked at me. "It's always the quiet ones you have to watch out for, huh?"

I raised an eyebrow at that. Logan had just got called up from our minor league affiliate, since we traded Jonesy for draft picks, and we needed to fill in the depth. None of us knew him well enough yet. Mac had taken him under his wing and gave him a place to stay while he was between the two hockey clubs.

I shrugged. "Maybe. She helps keep me in line."

"That's good for you. It's nice to find someone you can settle down with. Love's funny like that."

Whoa, love? I wasn't sure if I loved Maxine. The past couple of months with her have been great. Getting her out of her shell, and making her feel confident in the bedroom, had been awesome. I missed her so much when I was on the road. I craved her touch, her scent, and the feeling of her lithe body tucked against mine.

Was I in love?

I didn't think I'd ever been in love before. Not even with Natalie.

I gave him a light punch on the shoulder. "What about you, Cully?"

He sighed. "I don't have time for that shit. It's me and Liam against the world."

"Right, you have a kid."

He nodded solemnly. Logan was younger than me, so it was weird that the little rookie was a single dad. "My nephew, but yeah, I only have time for him and hockey."

"Not even time for a hookup? Come on, Cully, you need to get laid!"

"I'll bang a bunny once in a blue moon, but Liam comes first, always."

"Boys!" I yelled out. "Next road trip, Cully needs to get laid!"

Logan glared at me. "I'm fine."

"Nah, man, you'll be blocked up and playing like shit if you don't get it in."

Riley shook his head at me. "Christ, T, that's not a thing!"

"Yes, it is!" I argued.

Noah and Benny shook their heads at me, and I gave them all my lopsided smile. Okay, maybe it wasn't a thing, but Cully was wound too tight. And serious as shit. He needed to relax.

"Leave Cully alone," Riley said and nodded his head to the other guy. They had been playing on the same line since Jonesy got traded, and Riley was protective of his D pairing.

Logan shook his head and walked off to the showers. That kid was still a bit of a mystery.

"He's got a lot of shit on his plate," Noah said to me. "Don't turn him into you."

"But I'm so fun!" I joked.

Benny rolled his eyes. "More like a pain in the ass."

I flipped him the bird as he walked out, and I waited for Noah to finish fixing his hair. Benny didn't carpool with us because he slept at my sister's last night, but Noah and I had, since we were meeting the girls at the bar.

When we got to Eileen's, I jumped out of Noah's SUV, excited to see my girl again. "Come on, let's get a drink with our girls!" I urged.

He smiled at me. "I'm glad you found Max. She's good for you."

"Me too."

"But you owe me fifty bucks."

"Motherfucker, for what?" I protested.

The tall, pasty guy smiled. "You told me you were 'never gonna fall in love.' I'm calling bullshit right now."

"I'm not in love."

He pinned me with the stare he only used when he was on the face-off. Noah was the nicest dude you knew until you faced off with him on the ice. Canadian stereotype? That was Noah. When too nice Noah Kennedy pinned you with a death glare, you knew something was up.

"No? So you don't call your girl every night we're on the road?" he asked and gave me a smug grin. "And you're not thinking of her every time you aren't with her? And you don't smile when she sends you a text asking how your day is?"

I grumbled at him, but I pulled out my wallet and threw a couple of bills at him.

Dick.

"That doesn't mean I'm in love," I protested.

"Keep telling yourself that, bud."

When we walked into Eileen's, I spotted my girl across the room. She was wearing my jersey and tight jeans that hugged her nice ass. She looked sexy as hell, and I kinda wanted to fuck her in my jersey tonight.

I frowned when I saw she was talking to a big blonde dude who had his suit jacket rolled up to reveal a sleeve tattoo on one arm. Max tipped back her head and laughed at whatever he said to her. A spike of jealousy ran hot through my center at a man looking at my girl. She was *my* girl, nobody else's.

"Oh, hey, that's Holmstrom!" Noah said when he spotted them. Dinah was on the other side of the bar, so he was heading in the opposite direction.

"The dude we just beat?" I asked.

I was seeing red. Why was that asshole talking to my woman?

Noah arched an eyebrow at me. "Dude, chill. He's a homer."

"Blaise Holmstrom's from Philly?" I asked.

Noah shook my head at me. "Do you live under a rock? His dad owns the bar."

Oh.

Ohhhhh.

I knew Hal had two kids in the league, but I hadn't put two and two together with the name Holmstrom.

Noah walked over to Dinah, and I went in the other direction where Max was standing. I put my arms around her from behind. "Hey, you," she said with a big smile on her face when she looked up at me.

I kissed her cheek. "Hey, baby girl."

The possessive move did nothing to phase the blonde man she was talking to. Maybe I had misread the situation.

"Hey, do you know Blaise? We went to high school together," she introduced us with a warning look for me to behave.

I put out a hand to Blaise, and he firmly shook my hand. "I don't think we've met before, TJ Desjardins."

He laughed and rubbed his shoulder. "Nope, but you checked me hard into the boards tonight. Nice to see the Bulldogs hang around my dad's bar."

"Okay...how many Holmstroms are there?" I asked.

He laughed. "Six."

My eyes bulged out of my head.

Max laughed.

"Which one of you is the best hockey player? Surely not you," I teased.

He laughed. "Yeah, I'm kinda having a shit season. My long-time girlfriend broke up with me."

Max's face fell. "Oh, Blaise. I'm so sorry."

He shrugged. "I'll get over it. Eventually."

I cringed. "Sorry I brought it up."

He shook his head and ordered two more beers, and handed one to me. "Cheers, man. Oh, to answer your question, I think my sister's the best. She plays for U of T."

"Wow, she moved to Canada?" I asked.

He nodded. "She lives with me. We're pretty close."

I pointed to my sister, who was tipping back her head in a laugh while Benny kissed her neck from behind on the other side of the bar. "I get that. I have a twin sister. She's my best friend."

"No way! My sister's a twin too," he said.

Max's eyes were wide with excitement. "Hockey twins!"

157

I slid my eyes over to her empty glass of wine. "I think you had a little too much wine, eh, baby girl?"

She shrugged and gave me a sly smile. "Maybe..."

Blaise smiled at me. "You two are cute. I hate this being single shit."

I shrugged. "It can be fun, but yeah, it's nice to have your person."

Max slid her hand into mine at that, and I squeezed her tiny hand in my bigger one.

Blaise waved to one of his teammates who had walked in the door. He tipped his beer to me in salute. "That's one of my boys. It was nice meeting you. Let's get a drink the next time you play in Toronto, okay?"

We shook hands again. "Definitely, dude."

I thanked him for the beer, and I noticed Max typing away at her phone. I wrapped my arms around her waist and kissed her temple. She giggled against me, all girly like. Yup, she definitely had one too many glasses of wine tonight.

"What are you doing?" I asked her and nodded toward the phone in her hand.

She laughed. "Oh! Texting Blaise's younger brother Ayden to get the details on Blaise's situation."

"Why?"

"Because he's hot, and I'm sure I have a friend that would be interested in him."

My blood boiled at her saying another man was hot.

She must have seen the look on my face because she arched a blonde eyebrow at me. "Are you jealous?"

I took a swig of my beer. "No," I grumbled.

She looked up at me through her long lashes and bit her lip. "T?"

"Yeah, baby girl?"

Her cheeks were tinted pink, and then she got up on her tip-toes and pressed her lips to my ear. "You're the only man I'm taking home tonight."

I gave her my signature grin and pulled back to look at her. She was still biting her lip, and she dipped her head down, avoiding eye contact. I tipped up her chin with my finger. "You want me to take you home?"

She nodded.

"You gotta say the words, baby."

She blew out a breath.

Max had gone a long way from that awkward one-night stand in October. I loved that I helped her get over some of her apprehension in the bedroom, but sometimes she still didn't vocalize her needs. She'd avoid eye contact or not tell me what she really wanted. Sometimes I had to coax it out of her. That frustrated me because I was still terrified I wouldn't be enough for her. When I held her in my arms or kissed her, she made me feel safe and warm, and I never wanted those feelings to disappear. I had never felt this way before, but I was still so scared of ruining things.

"Please," she said.

"Please, what?"

She squeezed her eyes shut. "You're insufferable."

I grinned and cupped her face. "You want me to take you home?"

She snapped her eyes open and nodded.

"And then what?"

Her cheeks were bright red now. "I want to have loud marathon sex with you."

The corners of my lips tipped up into a grin. "Oh, really?"

"TJ!"

I held up my bottle of beer. "Hold on, baby, I gotta finish my beer."

She groaned. "T!"

I set my beer on the bar behind her. "Just kidding, baby. I want to fuck you all night long. Let's go."

Her face was still bright red, but I didn't miss the shy smile that curled up on her lips. My girl was still timid, but I could get her out of her shell, and I loved that about us.

CHAPTER TWENTY

MAXINE

I felt someone calling my name, but my mind was a blur. In front of me, smoke billowed from the engine of the car, and I was stuck in my seat. Beside me, Charlie had a huge gash on his forehead, but he wasn't moving when I tried to shake him awake. My parents were upfront, and they weren't responding, either.

Oh my god, my parents!

And then I was screaming.

"What's going on? Are you guys okay?" came a voice I couldn't quite place. A deep rumbling voice that wasn't TJ's. What the heck?

TJ whispered soft, comforting words into my ear as he cradled me in his arms. I clung to him and nuzzled my head into the crook of his neck. Crap, this was embarrassing. Why couldn't I stop these dreams from happening?

"Sorry, man. It's fine. Maxine just had a bad dream," TJ said while he rocked me in his arms and held me against his chest.

I slid my eyes open and saw Benny standing in the doorway of TJ's bedroom. His towering figure framed the door as he stood there, only wearing a pair of boxers. He obviously jumped out of bed at the sounds of my screams. I spied Rox peering behind him to see what was going on, her brow furrowed in concern.

I hated this. I didn't want to be this broken shell of a person anymore. I thought things were getting better; I hadn't even had a nightmare in a couple of weeks. TJ kept pressing me about going to therapy, but I kept telling him I'd 'think about it,' hoping he'd eventually drop it. I didn't see the point of rehashing the worst night of my life. What was even the point? They were all dead. Why did I get to live when they died?

I slid off of TJ's lap and started searching for my jeans. Rox and Benny shared a confused look but backed away out of the doorway.

"What are you doing?" TJ asked.

"I'm sorry. I'm gonna go," I mumbled.

I still couldn't find my jeans. Where were they?

"C'mere," he ordered.

I shook my head and dove to get my jeans, but TJ got to me first. He pulled me back onto the bed and into his lap. My face was stained with tears, but he wiped them away. I hated that he got to see me at my worst, that he saw all the damage I carried.

It was then I realized I had to set him free. He didn't want something complicated. He needed someone who could give themselves over to him, who would love him without bringing their emotional baggage into the relationship.

"Hey, look at me," he said and stroked the back of his finger across my cheek. "Talk to me, please."

"I think we should break up," I blurted.

He looked taken aback and hurt. "What did I do wrong?"

I shook my head. "You were perfect, but...I don't deserve you."

His hazel eyes softened, but his thumb brushed across my cheek in a soft caress. "No, Max, I'm the one who doesn't deserve you. I'm not a good boyfriend. I don't know how to help you."

I shook my head and tried to get out of his grasp, but he held onto my hips and kept me on his lap. "You shouldn't have to deal with my baggage. I'm broken, T, and that's never gonna change."

"Hey, you're not broken." he cooed softly and cupped my face, forcing me to look into his eyes.

"I should set you free, so you're not burdened with me anymore. You don't need this," I sobbed.

I hated being this emotional wreck in front of him all the time. I was always crying in his arms, and he tried so hard to be a good boyfriend by holding me tight and drying my tears. But it was unfair of me to expect him to keep doing that. He needed someone uncomplicated. Someone who didn't wake up screaming in their sleep. Someone who didn't have panic attacks at mere inconveniences.

He brushed a tear away. "Max, loving you isn't a burden. Christ, why do you think that? I love you and hate that I can't take these nightmares away from you."

I pulled back, my mouth agape at his admittance. "What?"

He looked up at me. "You know I love you, right?" He looked so earnest when he said it, like he had just come to the conclusion himself. He grabbed my hands and kissed the back of them. "You're the first person I think about when I wake up and the last person I think about when I go to sleep. You're the person I want to tell all my secrets to. And who I want at my side. I love you so much, but it kills me that I don't know how to help you."

"You love me?" I whispered.

My mind was going a mile by minute, and it couldn't process his words. My emotions were a raging storm inside. When he said the words, I felt they rang true, but my anxiety had me in a chokehold. How could this man love someone like me?

His lips curled up into a smile. "Yeah, I really do. I know you're not ready for that yet—"

"I love you too," I blurted out. "You know that, right? That's why I have to let you go."

"I'm not going anywhere, and you better learn that now," he growled.

"I'm sorry."

He ran his hands down my back soothingly. "I think you need to talk to someone. Will you do that for me? You said you'd think about it."

I shook my head. "I did. I'm not going."

He sighed. "I told you therapy helped me. I hate seeing you like this and knowing I can't chase away those nightmares. Will you go for me, please?"

I didn't want to talk about what happened that night. Ever. I didn't want to pour my soul out to some stranger with a Ph.D. That was all in the past, and I wanted my future to be with TJ. But I wasn't sure he would last much longer.

"How could you love someone as broken as me?" I choked out.

He made an annoyed noise in the back of his throat. "You're not broken. Who told you that?"

My jerk brain.

"No one."

He gritted his teeth and did that whole manly stiff upper lip thing. "Maxine, you're not broken. You just need a little help. I don't want to wake up every night to you screaming in terror. I think it could really help you. I'll even go with you."

I squeezed my eyes shut and shook my head.

I hated that he had to witness all my breakdowns and had to endure loving someone like me. But it still didn't mean I wanted to go see a therapist. That wasn't something that was ever done in my family. You kept those things to yourself. Strangers didn't need to know your business. I just wanted all of this stuff behind me and to move on.

"Please, baby? I love you, and I want to protect you and keep you safe. I can't keep you safe from those nightmares if you don't agree to do something about it," TJ urged.

When I looked into his eyes, it threw me at how scared he looked. This man loved me, but all I did was cause him pain.

"Think about it for real this time, okay, baby?" he pleaded.

"Okay," I whispered, relenting. I still didn't want to go, but when I looked at this man who loved me and only wanted the best for me, something inside me nagged at me to listen. "I promise I'll really think about it."

"That's all I ask," he whispered, and he leaned up to kiss me again. "Love you, but I have an early practice, so let's get back to bed, okay?"

"I'm sorry."

"S'okay."

No. It was not, but he wasn't going to admit it. The fact he wanted so badly for me to get better made me want to think about if therapy was a good idea. Keiana had been nagging me about it for a while, but I kept pushing her off. Maybe they both had a point.

I got off of TJ's lap and laid on my side instead while I mulled it over.

TJ pulled me tight against his chest and pulled the covers over us.

"It really helped you?" I asked.

"Yeah. Helped me get out of my head when I first got drafted."

I nodded and relaxed into his hold, letting myself really think about it. If it helped TJ, maybe he was right, and it could help me. But when his breathing got steady beside me, and he drifted off to sleep, panic coursed through me. I wasn't sure I'd ever be better. I didn't think telling some stranger all my problems would make all these feelings go away.

CHAPTER TWENTY-ONE

TJ

I woke up to Maxine's head on my chest as she curled her tiny body against mine. It was the best way to wake up, but unfortunately, I had to get to practice. I'd rather stay in bed all day long and cuddle with the girl I loved.

I frowned when I remembered the events of last night and why I told her I loved her. She had been so ready to take off and leave because she thought she was a burden, and I didn't like that.

My phone beeped on the bedside table, and I shifted her off me so I could turn it off. She stirred but didn't wake, which was good because she needed to sleep.

I kissed the top of her head while I rolled out of my bed and got dressed.

"Don't leave!" she whined sleepily. She slid one eye open as she watched me get dressed.

I smiled at her. "Sorry, baby. I have practice."

"I know. You have to stop taking too many penalties."

I laughed. "Sometimes I forget how much of a hardcore hockey fan you are."

"Sorry. I don't mean to be a nag. I'm sure you'll hear it during practice."

I kneeled on the bed and kissed her. "True, but I like listening to you more. Plus, you're cuter than Coach."

A blush crept up her pale face, and then she frowned. "I'm sorry about last night."

"I know, baby girl. I just want you to get better. I don't want to push you, but...seeing you that way breaks my heart. I don't know how to help you."

She scrubbed a hand down her face. "I hate making you feel that way. I'm sorry."

I kissed her forehead. "Don't break up with me again, okay?"

She nodded and hugged me tightly.

I wanted to ask her again if she was going to go to therapy, but I didn't want to push her. She promised she'd think about it, but I wasn't sure she actually would. I was afraid if I pushed more, she'd try to break up with me again. When she tried that last night, all my memories of why I didn't deserve her came crashing back over me. Like Natalie was in my head again, telling me I'd never be enough.

I kissed her goodbye but lingered on her lips.

"Babe, don't be late for practice," she said.

I cupped her face. "I love you, okay?"

Her smile lit up her whole face. "I love you too, so much."

"You better," I teased.

She rolled her eyes at me, and I walked out of the room.

In the kitchen, a similar scene occurred between my sister and my roommate. Benny hugged my sister to his chest, and he kissed the top of her head.

"You ready, man? Or are you gonna make more kissy faces at my sister?" I asked and made a grossed-out face.

They both gave me the finger, and Roxie kissed him goodbye one last time. Benny shrugged on his leather jacket, and we walked out of the condo together.

"Hey, man, is Max okay?" he asked when we got into the elevator. He stabbed the lobby button as soon as we stepped inside.

I shrugged and ran a hand through my hair. "Honestly? I don't know."

He stroked his beard. "I can ask my sister for a referral."

Benny's older sister was a therapist, but she worked with at-risk kids, so I didn't think that made sense for Max.

I chewed on my lip and stepped inside the elevator. I jabbed a finger at the garage level. "Maybe."

"Dude, that was scary last night. I thought it was Rox, and I freaked out. Are you okay?"

I sighed. "Not really. She tried to break up with me."

"Why?"

I shrugged. "She thinks she has to let me go, to unburden me with her baggage. But I'd pull down all the stars in the sky if she asked me to. I'd do anything for her."

Benny stared at me, his mouth hanging open for a moment, but then the elevator doors dinged open to the parking garage. "You love her, don't you?"

I nodded, and we walked together toward my car. "I've never felt this way before. I want to protect her, to keep her safe. It was hard leaving her this morning."

He nodded in understanding. "Yeah. Leaving Rox every morning sucks."

"I asked Max to talk to someone like your sister, but she said she'd think about it."

Benny stroked his beard. "She might need the extra push."

"I tried already, and I don't want her to try to break up with me again. I love her and want the best for her."

"You're so soft for her!"

A small smile played on my lips. "Yeah."

We climbed into my car, and I started the engine of my Maserati.

I got on the highway and headed to the practice facility on the Main Line. A lot of the guys kept moving to the suburbs, preferring to be closer to the practice facility. I liked living in the city, but if I ever got the two-point-five kids and the wife I always wanted, I'd consider moving too.

"Off-topic, but..." Benny cut into my thoughts after we had been driving in silence for a while. "I want to ask your sister something, and I want to run it by you."

"Bro, she doesn't believe in marriage," I reminded him.

"I know—neither do I. That's why she's perfect for me. I want to ask her to move in with me."

"You want to move out?"

"Dude, you don't want to hear me fuck your sister."

I shuddered, remembering how I found out about Benny and my sister dating. "True."

"And I don't want to hear you with your lady. We're both old enough that maybe we shouldn't have a roommate."

I nodded. I hated being alone. I got too into my head and doubted myself. But Benny had a point. I was old enough to be on my own. If he wanted to ask my sister to move in with him and start their life together, I wouldn't stand in his way. I wanted Rox to be happy, and Benny did that.

"When are you gonna ask her?"

He shrugged. "Soon. I'm looking at a place nearby I want to buy. What if she says no?"

I shook my head and drove into the parking lot of the practice facility. "She won't. Listen, my sister loves you. It took her a lot to get over you asking her rude questions, but honestly? I've been jealous of you."

"Me?" he asked.

I cut the engine of my Maserati and shook my head at him. "Not of you, specifically. Of what you have. What Noah and Dinah have, what Riley and Fi have. I thought I found it with Max, but she keeps pushing me away. Proving to me I'm just not good enough."

He peered at me with a curious look, and I got out of the car, already feeling like I had said too much. I hated being this vulnerable with anyone. Least of all, one of my teammates. I'd never hear the end of it.

Benny followed me into the facility, close on my heels. "You need her to know you're willing to fight for her. You need to prove that you have her back. If you don't want to put your heart on the line, if you don't want to help her wrestle her demons, you might as well sever your ties now."

"How do you help Rox with that?"

We walked into the locker room together, and I started stripping off my clothes and getting my gear on. Benny stripped his own clothes off and started wrapping the rainbow-colored tape around his stick.

He arched an eyebrow at me. "Usually, it helps when I get on my knees and spend a long time in-between her—"

I threw a towel at his head, and he laughed at me. "EW! I don't want to know that! I'm close with my sister, but I'm not *that* close."

Noah gave me a weird look as he pulled his practice jersey over his head. "Do I even want to know?"

Benny was still laughing to himself. Dick.

I shook my head. "Dude, you do not."

I got the rest of my gear on and skated out onto the ice beside Noah. We had been playing well, but I was nervous we wouldn't make the playoffs again. It wasn't like I had been slacking off. On the ice, I was skating my ass off, and when I was off it, I was watching a ton of game tape. And not just during practice either, but on my own time, too. I'd blame Riley for that; that dude was such a stats fiend, it was growing on the rest of us.

During practice, I compartmentalized my unsure feelings about my girlfriend's mental health and focused on what I was doing on the ice. I went through our drills while we were on the ice, and I sat attentively in our team meetings afterward. I laughed when the assistant coach gave me some shit about too many PIMs lately. I couldn't wait to tell Max and hear her laugh about it.

After we spent some time reviewing game tape, we went into the weight room to get more strength training in. Noah had been on me lately that we needed to be faster, bigger, and stronger on the ice if we wanted to make the playoffs. He was hungry for the cup this year.

Benny and Riley were doing squats while I spotted Noah at the bench press.

"Is Max still having those night terrors?" he asked.

I groaned. "Yeah."

"Dinah woke me up last night because we heard her screams."

I sighed. "Sorry. It scared the fuck out of Roxie and Benny."

"She okay?" he asked while he finished his set and put the barbell back on the rack.

"Not really. And she tried to break up with me."

"You're okay now, though, right?"

I shrugged and laid on the bench to run through a set while he spotted me. "I think so. She didn't seem happy when I told her she should go to therapy."

"It's not a bad idea. D went to therapy after her husband died. She was really lost after that, and I know it helped her a lot. You want me to have her talk to Max?"

I shook my head. I was pretty sure that would have scared Max off even more.

I didn't think going to therapy was weak. Like I told her, I had a sports psychologist when I was a rookie and struggling to find my footing. My dad suggested it because he went to one after his career prematurely ended. He was one of those rare old-school hockey guys who thought mental health was just as important as physical health. So, of course, I'd thought it would help my girlfriend. I wished she wasn't being so stubborn about it.

"I told her I loved her," I blurted out when I finished my set.

A big grin spread across Noah's face. "Called it!"

I sat up and wiped the sweat off my brow. "Shut it!"

"What did she say?"

"That's when she tried to break up with me!"

Noah frowned. "Why?"

I sighed. "Because she thinks she's a burden, but bro, I love that woman, and I want to keep her safe."

"I get that. I feel the same way about D. But are you guys okay, though?"

I nodded. "Yeah, she said she loves me too, and she'll think about therapy again, but I think she just told me that so I'd stop pestering her."

Noah and I switched positions so I could spot him again. "Maybe she will this time. But maybe you don't press her too hard? I live with a stubborn woman who doesn't want anyone to tell her what to do, so believe me, being subtle can be key."

He had a point. I said what I needed to say to Max last night; I just hoped it resonated with her. I hoped she realized I wasn't trying to 'fix her,' but I just wanted to take that pain away.

After we finished our training session, we went back into the locker room to grab our stuff. I checked my phone, and a grin spread across my face when I saw a message from Max.

BABYGIRL: *Come over for dinner tonight? I'll make your favorite!*

ME: *[cat emoji][tongue emoji]*

BABYGIRL: *Not that you perv!*

ME: *You love me!*

BABYGIRL: *I do! I'm making the lasagna you love.*

ME: *Sounds perfect. I'll see you soon.*

Noah nudged me.

"What?"

He gave me a cocky grin. "Now there's a man in love!"

I grinned because I couldn't argue with that. Things might not be perfect with Max right now, but it didn't change how she felt like my home.

CHAPTER TWENTY-TWO

MAXINE

I finished placing the last layer on my lasagna when my phone beeped again. I thought it was TJ again, but I frowned when I saw it was from Benny.

BENNY: *Hey, TJ will be mad about this, but...here's my sister's number. She might have someone to refer you to.*

I clenched my teeth as I reread his text message.

I told TJ last night I would really think about talking to someone this time, but that didn't mean he needed to get Benny involved.

Keiana walked into the kitchen and saw the annoyed look on my face. She froze in her tracks. "What's wrong?"

I sighed. "TJ wants me to go talk to someone."

She waved her hand to make me elaborate.

"About my night terrors," I said.

She raised her eyebrows. "Oh. Wow. Maxine, I've been telling you should have done that years ago."

"I don't want to unearth everything about my parents and Charlie. It's in the past."

She hugged me. "Aw, honey. I know. But you should have gone right after it happened. I know this is hard for you, but it's scary when you get like that."

I chewed my bottom lip. "It really upset him."

"Yeah?"

"I tried to break up with him last night."

"Why?"

I sighed. "He doesn't deserve to put up with me."

Keiana narrowed her eyes. "Did he say those things?"

"No. And then..." I trailed off.

She nudged me. "Then what?"

"He told me he loved me. I was trying to break up with him, but he told me he loved me and was worried about me."

She slapped my arm. "Max! Don't let that man go."

"I don't want to bring him down with all my baggage."

She gave me a hard look. It was the look she gave me when I was being purposefully obtuse.

"He obviously cares about you, and all this stuff you hold inside is really scaring him. I know you don't like talking about the accident, but you need to." She went over into the junk drawer and searched for a bit before she pulled out a business card and handed it to me. "You know I work in the medical field, right? I know people."

I pocketed the card but didn't make the call. I wasn't ready for that yet. I didn't want to go to therapy at all. Keiana had been on me to go for years, but now that TJ was urging me to do it too, I felt like I was getting it at all angles.

"Max, it would really help you," Keiana said.

I chewed on my lip. "I'm scared."

She gave me another hug. "I know. But if TJ sees how much you need the help too, maybe it's time."

I blew out a breath, and Keiana gave my arm a little

squeeze. She walked out into the living room, letting the conversation drop.

I thought about what Keiana and TJ said while I put the lasagna in the oven. I tried to shake my thoughts away, but they dug inside my heart, telling me to listen to them. They both wanted what was best for me. Maybe I should consider it.

I went into the living room to join Keiana. "You off tonight?" I asked.

She nodded. "I've got a date."

"Oh, yeah? Anyone I know?"

She shook her head. "This hot surgeon. I've heard he's kind of a douche, but if he's good in bed, I don't care."

I felt my cheeks getting pink, and it went all the way to my ears. Even though I had gotten more comfortable with sex stuff, I kept that in the bedroom. I still couldn't say a lot of stuff outside of it without blushing. Sometimes, I thought Keiana said stuff like that to get a rise out of me.

She laughed. "You should see your face. I thought you were getting over that stuff."

"I am, but it's still awkward for me sometimes."

"Sorry, I don't mean to make you uncomfortable."

I fixed her with a glare. She was my best friend, so I knew she was full of it. She gave me a cheeky grin back.

We watched TV while I waited for the lasagna to cook. I wanted to make dinner extra special tonight since I felt bad about what happened last night.

After a little while, Keiana stood up from the couch. "I better get ready for my date."

After she went upstairs, I pulled the business card Keiana gave me out of my pocket and looked at the name and contact info. I tapped a finger against my lip and stared at it until my eyes went crossed.

I needed to do this, but I didn't want to. I needed to get better. I just didn't want to unearth all the pain and guilt I'd felt after the accident. Seeing TJ so upset last night was still clear in my mind. I hated that he saw my panic attacks and had to deal with my terrifying nightmares. But he loved me, and I'd promised him I'd think about it. And this time, I wasn't lying so he'd stop pestering me about it.

I blew out a nervous breath and took out my phone. It was now or never. I typed the email address into my email app and composed a quick message. Maybe one little meeting would help me sort out my issues. I hoped it was enough to disentangle the guilt wrapped around me.

I watched the TV blankly until the timer for my lasagna went off. I enjoyed cooking for TJ. I liked being a caregiver to him and being the person he leaned onto after a bad game.

I was plating the lasagna when I heard a knock on the door. I went to open it, and my heart did jumping jacks when I saw my boyfriend standing behind it, giving me that classic Desjardins smirk.

"Hey, baby girl," he greeted.

I smiled at him and let him inside. He took off his boots and shuffled out of his coat and joined me inside. He raked some flurries out of his hair. "Is it snowing?" I asked.

"These flurries are nothing," he scoffed as he plunked down onto a chair in the kitchen. He caught me by the waist before I could go back into the kitchen and bring in our plates. I laughed, and he curled his hands into my hair while he kissed me.

I melted into him but pulled away before he pulled me upstairs. "Hey. Food's gonna get cold. You have perfect timing."

"Don't care—needed to kiss you. I missed you."

I laughed. "You saw me this morning."

He pressed his forehead against mine. "I know, but I'm about to go on another road trip."

I slid off his lap, despite his frown, and went to get our plates. I put his plate down in front of him, and he thanked me before devouring it. Damn, hockey players could put it away. Maybe next time, I needed to double that recipe. At Thanksgiving, I thought we would have leftovers since I went a little overboard with all the food, but he and Benny had scarfed all of it down.

I shook my head with a laugh as TJ shoveled food into his face. My phone buzzed against the table, and when I glanced at the notification, the hair on the back of my neck stood up when I saw a response to my email.

Hi, Maxine.

Sounds like you could use someone to talk to. Please call my office as soon as you can, and we can set up a time for our first session. Looking forward to working together.

-Dr. Rebecca Brown

TJ nudged me with his foot. "What's wrong?"

I shook my head. "Nothing wrong. I'm—I'm setting up an appointment with a therapist."

His face lit up into a big smile. "Baby, I'm so proud of you."

"I didn't go yet," I grumbled.

He reached a hand across the table and grabbed my smaller one in his. He rubbed his thumb across the back of my hand in a soothing gesture. "I know, but I'm proud that you're taking the steps. I hate seeing you like that. I want to keep you safe and happy."

I grinned at him. "You do!"

He grinned back. "Thank you for making me dinner. That was nice."

"I enjoy doing that. I like taking care of you."

I cleared our plates but gasped when I felt his hands wrap around my waist from behind and his lips on the nape of my neck. He pushed my hair off my shoulder and kissed up to my ear, forcing a shiver to go down my spine.

"I hate that I have to fly out tomorrow," he whispered in my ear.

I let the plates soak in the sink and washed my hands. I shook them out, which elicited a 'hey' from TJ as I flicked water droplets onto him. I turned in his arms and grinned at him. "Sorry, baby."

He caressed my cheek with his hand and rubbed his calloused thumb across my skin. I shamelessly leaned into his hand. Our relationship was akin to a long-distance one, so I learned to take advantage of the precious time we had together. Rox warned me how hard it could be with our men away all the time. I didn't realize how much until I started dating her brother.

"I'm sorry my job keeps me away from you," he offered.

"I would never ask you to change your job. You love playing hockey. It sucks, but I get it."

"You're the best. How did I get so lucky with you?"

I shrugged but snaked my hands around his neck. "Lucky? You chased me. After I went home with you, I never imagined you would become my boyfriend."

He bent his head, slanting his lips against mine in a quick kiss. His eyes twinkled in delight when he pulled away from me. I could stare into those swirls of greens and browns forever.

"Yeah, I guess I kind of did," he said. "I'm still not sure if I'm a good boyfriend. I feel like we're in a constant state of stealing moments together."

"S'okay, baby. I understand hockey's your life, and your

job's important to you. You love what you do, and I love watching you excel at it," I reassured him.

We pulled away when we heard the clomping of Keiana's high heels on the steps. TJ peered out of the kitchen doorway, and I did the same. She laughed at our twin expressions. Keiana was wearing her typical slinky black date dress with stilettos. She looked gorgeous, as always.

She walked into the kitchen with a smile. "Too much?" she asked and did a little spin.

"Perfect!" I hyped her up.

"Looking hot, Kei!" TJ said.

She pinned me with an amused stare. "You better watch your man, Max. I might steal him."

TJ put his arm around my waist, pulling me to his side. "Nah, she has me wrapped around her little finger."

"You two are so cute! I can't stand it!" Keiana squealed.

"Hey, did you want to eat? There's leftover lasagna," I said.

Keiana and TJ rolled their eyes together. "Max, you're such a mom!"

I laughed. "I can't help it! I like taking care of people."

I pretended I didn't see TJ mouth 'mother hen' to my best friend. They were only teasing because they both loved it. I didn't think it was a bad thing.

Keiana went into the kitchen and made herself a plate from the leftover lasagna. It honestly surprised me there were any leftovers with how much TJ could eat. She moaned as she ate it over the kitchen island.

"Max, this is so good," she said.

"Oh, not my creation. I got the recipe from Dinah."

"Really?" TJ asked with a raised eyebrow. "D doesn't cook much."

I shrugged. "I think it's from her brother. I just followed the recipe. It's not like it's hard."

"Says you!" Keiana argued.

I shrugged. Cooking wasn't that hard, as long as you could follow directions. Keiana looked at TJ. "Are you guys going to make the playoffs this year?" she asked.

He ran a hand through his thick, dark hair. "We're trying. I have high hopes, but you never know."

"Defense has been good since Cully and Riley paired up. I'm pulling for you," she said.

TJ gave her an amused look. "You two know a scary amount about hockey."

Keiana laughed. "We spent a lot of time watching the hockey team in high school. Also, we're diehard Bulldogs fans!"

I nodded. "This is true."

TJ laughed and kissed my temple again. "I wouldn't have it any other way."

Keiana cleared her plate and put it in the sink. "Okay, kids. I gotta jet, don't do anything I wouldn't do."

She was out of the house before I could mention that wasn't much. I didn't wonder about that, because I spent the rest of the evening in bed with my boyfriend, anyway.

CHAPTER TWENTY-THREE

TJ

My eyes darted back and forth between Noah and the lumbering San Jose Vipers forward he was facing off against. He won the face-off and flicked the puck my way. I sped down the ice, taking the puck up past the blue line, and passed it back to Benny. He stick-handled it out of the way of the San Jose defenseman and flicked it back to Noah. Noah took the shot, but it went off the post. It all happened so fast that I didn't even groan because I scrambled to get the rebound before the goalie covered it with his glove. Muscle memory took over, and I jabbed it with my stick, and then the arena went dead silent.

The lamp behind the goaltender lit up.

HOLY FUCK.

That actually went in.

Noah hugged me on the ice, and I skated down the bench, high-fiving my teammates, before opening the gate to join them. Noah fist-pumped me while I gulped down a sports drink and tried to catch my breath.

"Come on, boys!" our captain cheered from behind the bench.

I watched with bated breath, chewing on my mouth guard while Hallsy had possession of the puck. The San Jose netminder had a weak five-hole, and Hallsy was trying to capitalize on that.

I groaned with the rest of my team when his shot hit the post and the opposing defenseman slapped it down the ice. I shared a nervous look with Noah. If we held them off for a few more minutes, we could win the game. The home fans were cheering on San Jose, but if we focused on the game in front of us, we could still win.

The crowd booed when Hallsy won the face-off and attempted to set up another play. He took the shot, and it landed top right shelf.

"Did that go in?" Noah asked me.

The lamp behind the goalie lit up red, and then our whole bench was standing up and cheering on our guys. There was his answer—3-1 us with fifty seconds left on the clock.

Coach tapped me on the helmet, and I hopped over the bench for the change-up. I took the face-off, but I went too quickly, and the ref kicked me out. Benny replaced me and won, trying to set something else up. We couldn't let them get another scoring chance.

We ended up battling with San Jose until the siren sounded. 3-1 FINAL.

I danced into the visitors' locker room. "That's how we do it, boys!" I cheered as Riley turned on the stereo for our victory game song.

Noah shook his head at me as he stripped his jersey off. Winning always amped me up. And made me horny. Too bad my girl was thousands of miles away.

After talking to the media and getting a shower, I was tying my tie at my cubby, waiting for Noah to do the same. He was too busy texting on his phone and taking his sweet time.

"Bro, come on!" I whined.

I swear he went slower. "What's your damage?"

"We're getting drunk tonight, and you're taking forever!"

Noah shook his head and finally hurried his ass up so we could get to the bus outside.

When we made it back to the hotel, Noah, Benny, Riley, and I headed to the bar. I ordered an expensive scotch, and we all got hammered. Except for Benny because he was such a lightweight and was still nursing his beer.

I snapped a picture of him and sent it to my sister.

ME: *Your man has been drinking this beer for an hour!*

ROXIE: *HAHA! He's so weak.*

ME: *How did you end up with such a lightweight?*

ROXIE: *More beer for me! But also, who told that man he's allowed to wear that suit like that?? Ugh, he's so hot.*

ME: *EW!*

ROXIE: *HAHA. Sorry dude, don't text me hot pictures of my man. Buy him another beer and give him shit for me?*

ME: *ALWAYS!*

I didn't have to buy him a drink, though, because Riley bought a round of shots for the table.

Riley nudged his best friend. "Come on, dude, drink up. You've been nursing that beer like a college freshman at their first party. We've got shit to celebrate!"

Benny made a face. "It was one game. It's not like we're in the playoffs yet."

"Not yet! But we needed that win, boys!" I cheered.

Noah clinked glasses with me. "Fucking right!" Then a

serious look came across his face. "Can I ask you guys something?"

I arched an eyebrow at him. "What's up?"

"I asked Dinah's brothers for permission."

"Permission for...oh!" Riley exclaimed, and his eyes widened at the realization. "Dude, don't tell me that. I can't keep that shit from Fi."

"Is it too soon?" Noah asked and stroked his beard nervously.

"Nah!" I said. "If you hadn't taken so long to make a move, you'd probably already be married by now."

"What if she says no?"

Riley and Benny shook their heads in unison. "No way, man. She loves you," Benny said.

I squeezed his shoulder. "Yeah, dude, it's gonna be great. How are you gonna do it?"

He smiled. "Probably take her to that Thai place she loves and ask her there. Is that too cliché?"

Riley shrugged. "Don't look at me. After that douche nozzle left Fi at the altar, I asked her if she wanted to marry a different groom. To which she said YOLO."

I laughed. "You never told us that!"

He shrugged. "I like to keep some things a mystery."

"I can't help you. I'm never getting married," Benny said and shuddered.

"What about you, T? What would you do?" Noah asked.

"Wine and dine and sixty-nine her," I said with a cheeky grin.

That made Benny and Riley howl with laughter while Noah glared at me. He should have been used to my antics by now.

"Be serious! I don't know how to ask her."

"I'm serious. Maybe take her to that fancy vegan place and have some good wine, but I wouldn't ask her in the restaurant. Maybe in Rittenhouse Square Park? Or later at home? She wouldn't like a public proposal," I rattled off.

All three heads cocked at me.

"What?" I asked and finished my scotch.

Noah poked me. "Do you mean *Max* would like that?"

I froze. Yeah, I was thinking about Max in particular and not in a hypothetical scenario. Hence mentioning the fancy vegan place.

Max wouldn't like a public proposal. My shy girlfriend wouldn't want to be the center of attention.

Holy fuck. Do I want to marry Max?

Maybe. I loved her, and I would do anything for her. She was the first person I thought about when I woke up and the last person I thought about as I was falling asleep. She had stolen my heart, and I didn't want it back.

"Maybe someday, but we haven't been together that long. I gotta get her to stop trying to break up with me first."

"That shit was scary, dude. I thought it was Rox, and I..." Benny trailed off. "She was screaming bloody murder. It scared the shit out of me."

"She thinks she needs to let me go," I said.

Noah looked thoughtful. "She doesn't want to burden you with her pain."

I groaned. "But I want her to! I want her to know she can lean on me."

"Dude, she knows that," Benny said.

"South Philly women, man. They're stubborn!" Noah joked.

"I don't think it's just the Philly women," Riley chimed in. "I got one of those, and she's from Minnesota."

"Do we all have a type?" Noah asked with a laugh.

Benny squinted at him and held his finger and thumb together. "Maybe. She'll figure it out. You just have to be there for her. Let her know that you're not going anywhere. Fight for her."

I nodded. He was right, but right now, I didn't want to talk about my concerns with Max's mental health.

I shifted the conversation back to Noah's proposal. "Wasn't your first date at her brother's pizza shop?"

Noah nodded. "Yeah, but I think she would be mad if I did it there. Frankie would text the family group chat immediately."

I laughed. "No matter how you do it, she'll say yes. She loves you."

He bit his lip. "I hope so."

"Oh dude, I got it!" Riley exclaimed.

"What?" Noah asked.

"Build her a bookshelf."

I squinted at Riley in thought.

"Shirtless," Riley said as he took another sip of his drink. "She won't be able to look away."

I laughed. "Are you suggesting he thirst trap D into a proposal?"

Noah was stroking his beard in thought. "It's not a completely terrible idea. I'll put it in the 'maybe' column."

We had a couple more rounds, and Benny got really drunk, which was hilarious. He was one of the biggest guys on the team, but he couldn't hold his liquor. We always gave him shit for it, and it would never stop being funny to me.

My vision swam when I got back to my hotel room. I took a shower to mellow out before crawling into bed and video chatting with Max.

I smiled when her face showed up on my phone screen.

She gave me that sweet smile. "Hey, baby. You look a little worse for wear."

"Hey, baby girl. Fuck, it's late," I said.

She laughed. "S'okay. It's a weekend, remember?"

"I don't even know what day it is," I admitted.

"You seem tipsy, baby. Why don't I let you go to sleep, and I'll see you tomorrow when you get home, okay?"

"I wanted to see your face and hear your voice before I went to bed. I miss you."

She smiled sweetly again. "I miss you too."

"How did the appointment go?"

She frowned. "It's tomorrow."

"You want me to go with you?"

She shook her head. "You won't be back by then."

I frowned. "Okay...you're gonna go, right?"

She clenched her jaw. She didn't want to talk about this, but I was worried about her. "Told you I would."

I nodded and tried not to frown. I didn't want her to be tormented by her past anymore, but it was so frustrating how she shut down when I suggested she get help.

She sighed. "We'll talk about this when you get back, okay? I'm sorry, I'm being difficult. You played awesome tonight!"

"You know how you can make it up to me?" I asked.

"How?"

I gave her my lopsided grin. "We can have a sexy video chat."

She tipped back her head and laughed. "You're ridiculous!"

"What's ridiculous about that?"

I was only teasing her. I knew it wasn't something she was comfortable with. I was just trying to lighten the mood and see her smile again.

She bit her lip like she was actually thinking about it for a moment. "Okay," she whispered.

I must have been too drunk because I didn't think I heard her right. Then I nearly dropped my phone when she took off her shirt.

"Baby girl," I groaned.

"What?" she asked. "This is what you wanted, right?"

Yes. Fuck, yes. I missed those tits so much, and my dick was so hard it hurt. But I didn't think she was comfortable with video chat sex.

"Only if you're comfortable with this. I was just teasing."

"Um..." She trailed off, and her cheeks got pink. "We both know you were not. But..."

"But what, baby?"

She blew out a nervous breath. "You make me feel comfortable with sex. I love that you always check in to make sure I'm good with something. Like right now, I know you're so horny, but you made sure I was good with this first."

I nodded. "You're more important to me. I want to make you feel comfortable."

"I am..." Her voice dropped to a low whisper. It was cute how she still got embarrassed by her own arousal. But I loved that I helped her feel free about her sexuality. It was a huge turn-on. "You need to guide me on this."

I slid my boxers off and gripped my dick. I hadn't expected her to agree to this, but I loved that she was willing to try it.

"Spread those legs and let me see," I said, my voice thick with my arousal.

"Okay," she said meekly and slipped her panties off.

I pumped my dick as I stared at her naked body. "Touch yourself like your hands are mine."

She spread her legs and slipped her hand down between her legs. She tipped back her head and moaned.

"That's a good girl. You're just as horny as me."

She whimpered and then opened her eyes. "I miss your big hands on me. Pumping inside me or pressing me against the bed while you take me from behind."

"Fuck," I groaned, and my hand moved faster. "Be a good girl and come all over your hand, just for me."

Her hand moved faster on her clit. She arched her back and angled her phone, so I could see her laid out for me while she pleasured herself as if I was right there with her. I stroked my dick faster and watched her.

"TJ!" she moaned, and I couldn't hold off any longer. I blew my load into my hand while I watched her body writhe as she came.

I set my phone down to clean myself up, and when I came back to it, Max had obviously done the same thing because she was dressed in her pajamas again.

She played with the hem of her shirt. "Was I...good?"

"Yeah, baby, you were good. I've never done that before."

"Really?"

I nodded. "Only for my baby girl."

Her smile grew bigger, and it hit me square in the chest.

"Love you, T. Now go to sleep!"

"Night, baby. Can't wait to get home and have you in my arms."

CHAPTER TWENTY-FOUR

MAXINE

I stared at the clock and watched the hand tick the seconds away. Then I turned back to Dr. Rebecca Brown. Rebecca was a lanky woman with light brown skin and curly dark hair who stared back at me with an open expression that let me know I was calling the shots. We had been sitting here in silence for five minutes already, and she hadn't pressed me to say anything yet.

I toyed with the hem of my skirt. "So do I start, or do you?"

She uncapped and recapped her pen and set her notebook down. "You called me. So why don't you tell me why you made the appointment?"

I closed my eyes and sighed.

How did I explain it to her? I made the appointment because the nightmares scared my boyfriend. Waking up to me screaming in my sleep made him worry too much. Because he loved me, but I didn't think he deserved the baggage I came with.

"Maxine, you don't have to tell me anything you don't want to. This is a safe space," she said in a soft voice.

I crossed my legs and uncrossed them again, and tried to will the words out of me. I would rather melt into the couch than tell her why I came here. I didn't want to talk about the accident. Or how Charlie and my parents' death still tormented me after all these years.

Rebecca sat back in her chair and offered me a small smile, but she didn't repeat her question. She was waiting for me to make the first move, but nerves wrapped around my chest so tight I couldn't get the words out.

The tick-tick-tick of the hand on the clock felt like it was booming across the room as we sat in silence. I promised TJ I would try therapy, that I'd try to talk to someone, and Rebecca seemed nice, but I wasn't sure I could do this.

I let out a heavy breath and then did it again. When it happened one more time, I realized I was hyperventilating.

Crap.

"Maxine, are you okay?" Rebecca's voice penetrated through my murky thoughts.

My vision blurred, and tears pricked my eyes. "No," I squeaked out. "I'm having a panic attack."

She reached out and put a hand on my leg. "Breathe, okay? Can you do that for me?"

I nodded and squeezed my eyes shut. I focused on my breathing and tried to calm myself down.

"You don't have to tell me anything you don't want to."

I wiped the tears from my eyes. "I don't think I'm ready yet."

She gave me a small smile and handed me a box of tissues. "That's okay. We can go at your pace, but I'd like to know what prompted your visit today. If you're open to that."

I dabbed at my eyes with the tissue and swallowed hard.

I didn't know if I could do this. I already had a panic attack, and I hadn't told her a single thing about why I was here.

"No pressure. If you want to sit here in silence until you're ready, we can do that too."

I nodded and let her words sink into me.

I wanted to get better, but thinking about that night made me want to run away and never speak to anyone ever again.

Rebecca and I sat in silence for a few more minutes. My breathing had gone back to normal, but I still fiddled with the hem of my skirt, unsure where to start. She had a patient smile on her face while she waited for me to speak up again.

I straightened up my spine and took a deep, calming breath. "I have night terrors."

Rebecca picked up her notepad and wrote something down.

"About the accident that killed my parents and my boyfriend when I was eighteen."

She nodded her head. "Do you want to talk about it today?"

I shook my head.

"That's okay, Maxine. We can figure this out together."

"Okay," I said meekly.

"Have you seen someone before? After the accident?"

I shook my head.

"Did something make you want to talk to me today?"

"My boyfriend. I wake up screaming at night, and he's worried about me. He wants me to get better, but I don't know how."

"The fact you came here today is a big step. It's okay to admit when you need help, and that's what I'm here for." She set her notepad and pen down again and crossed her legs. "Tell me about your boyfriend."

"He's not what I expected. He's a professional athlete; they tend to have a certain..." I paused for a moment. I wasn't sure it was polite to say TJ was a playboy before we came into each other's lives, even if it was the truth. "I'm his first serious girlfriend since high school. But he's the one who pushed me to make the appointment."

"Why do you think he did that?"

I cringed. "Because I keep trying to break up with him."

She sat up straighter. "Why's that?"

I waved off her alarmed look. "Oh, nothing like that! I feel like a burden, and he doesn't deserve to be with someone so broken."

"Did he say that?"

"No."

"Then why do you think that?"

I shrugged.

"Has he ever made you feel like you were a burden to him?"

Well, no. He made mistakes with me before we got together, but even then, he never made me feel like I didn't deserve his love. That had all been my jerk brain, telling me I wasn't worthy.

"No. He tries so hard to be a good boyfriend," I explained.

"He sounds like he really cares about you."

I nodded. "He does."

"What sport does he play?" she asked.

"Hockey."

She frowned. "Are you a big hockey fan? I don't know anything about that."

I nodded. "Diehard. I work for the team."

"What's that like?"

I spent the next few minutes explaining hockey to her and admitted that I loved working for the team but didn't love my actual job. She pressed me on that, and I told her my worries about my boss being TJ's sister, so I couldn't tell him how I really felt about it. She asked me pointed questions about what I wanted to do instead, but I didn't have an answer.

I realized when I looked at the clock and saw our time was almost up that she had been trying to get me to open up by asking about hockey and my job. She was trying to dig her way inside my brain so she could unlock the rest of my secrets later.

Rebecca peered up at the clock on her wall. "Listen, Maxine, that's our time for today. But I think we have a lot of things we still need to discuss. I'd like to see you weekly if that works for you?"

I stood up and shook her hand. "Thank you for meeting with me today. I'm not..." I let out a shaky breath. "I'm not ready to talk about everything yet. It's all too painful."

"We'll get there in time, but I'm glad you finally decided it was time to get help. There's no shame in needing that. We can talk more about your career troubles later, too."

I frowned.

I didn't want to talk about that either. I hated my job, but I tried to keep that to myself. I never knew if TJ might let it slip to his sister how unhappy I was. He knew it wasn't my passion, and I didn't exactly like it, but I didn't admit to him how much I hated it. I was afraid of that getting back to his sister, and then I'd get fired.

"Or not, if you don't want to," she said. "We can talk about whatever you want in these sessions. I want them to be comfortable for you."

I nodded. "Okay. I'll see you next week."

I waved to her on my way out, then walked down to the parking garage and got into my car.

I felt drained from talking about my issues. I wanted to go home and curl up in my bed. TJ got home from his road trip today, but I hadn't seen him yet. Tomorrow was game day, so I wanted to see him tonight, but I was emotionally exhausted.

I looked at my phone and furrowed my brow at the text message from the man in question.

TJ: *Come to Roxie's game!*

As much as I loved Rox, I didn't want to do that. I wanted to be in my bed, preferably with TJ by my side.

ME: *Babe, I'm exhausted. I want to go home.*

TJ: *Party Pooper! Come on! Come watch her kick ass and take names.*

I smiled at that. Rox killed it on the ice in her beer league. She didn't want to hear it, but she should play for the PHF. It was too bad they didn't have a Philly team. If Philly got a team, I might have put more pressure on her to play for the league instead.

My phone vibrated in my hand and alerted me of another text. It wasn't another text from TJ, though; this one was from Benny.

BENNY: *Come watch my lady play! Your boy's being all pouty because he misses you but also wants to support his sister.*

ME: *It really is like dating both of them, huh?*

BENNY: *Get used to it, girl!*

I put my phone back into my purse and drove over to

the rink. Finding parking was annoying, but after finding a garage, I walked over. I was hungry, and I hadn't eaten dinner yet. I guess something at the concession stands would do.

It was already the second period when I walked inside the small rink that Rox's beer league team played at. I spied her speeding down the ice on the breakaway almost immediately. She blew everyone else on the ice out of the water. I went up to the concessions and ordered nachos with cheese that I was eighty-five percent sure wasn't real. Didn't care—it was still delicious.

It didn't take me that long to find everyone. Benny was standing up and yelling at the refs while TJ was shouting coaching tips to his sister. I spied Noah and Dinah seated next to them. Noah looked beet red with embarrassment, but Dinah looked like she was loving it.

I took my seat next to Dinah. "Hey," I greeted around a mouthful of nachos.

She smiled at me. "Hey! We need to corral those two."

I waved my hand away. "Let 'em be. I want to eat in peace."

"Oh, come on, that's holding!" Benny yelled.

"Dudes! Sit down!" Noah chastised. "You're gonna get us kicked out."

"Again," Dinah muttered.

TJ turned around and saw me. I waved as I shoved more nachos in my mouth. I didn't want to rehash how my appointment went with him. He came over and sat beside me.

He tried to kiss me, but I gave him my cheek. "Stop, I'm eating."

"I missed you," he said and pouted.

I swallowed my food. "Missed you too."

He stole a tortilla chip, and I swatted his hand away but let him take it. "How did it go?" he asked.

I shook my head.

"Bad?"

"I don't want to talk about it."

I watched the muscles in his jaw tick, and I knew he was trying to hold his tongue. "You're gonna continue to go, though, right?"

"Yes," I gritted out and ignored him to watch his twin sister on the ice.

TJ put a hand on my leg and squeezed it through the tights I wore under my skirt. I warmed at his touch. I loved when he rested his hand on my thigh like that because it made me feel protected. The small gesture told me I was his, and he would always be there for me.

I realized I was being pissy with TJ for no reason. I opened my mouth to apologize, but it died on my lips when Dinah exclaimed, "Holy fuck!"

I watched the ice, but it was a shift change, and nothing too exciting was happening yet. "What's wrong?" I asked.

"Philly got a PHF team," she said.

Benny turned around at that. "Seriously?"

"Dude, yes!" Dinah almost screamed. "We HAVE to convince Rox she needs to try out!"

Benny got a wild look in his eyes. "Yes!"

"Roxie would kick ass in that league, but she won't do it," TJ argued.

I finished my dinner and got up to throw the paper container away in the trash. When I came back to our seats, I stood next to Benny in front of the glass and watched Rox on the ice.

"She's afraid playing in the pro league would make it

harder on your relationship. It's already so difficult with you guys on the road all the time," I explained to Benny.

"But they don't travel as much!" he argued.

I poked him in the chest. "I agree, but you gotta convince her. She's wiping the ice with everyone tonight. She needs to be playing at a higher caliber."

I walked back over to where TJ was sitting, and he pulled me into his lap. I wrapped my arms around his neck and kissed him. Sparks always flew when TJ kissed me but especially after he'd been on the road.

I pulled away and rested my forehead against his. "Hi."

He gave me the famous Desjardins smirk. "Hey, baby girl."

"You wanna get out of here?"

He slid me off his lap. "Bye!" he called to his friends while he dragged me out of the rink.

That made me laugh. So much for wanting to support his sister.

We spent the rest of the night in each other's arms, and it distracted TJ enough that he didn't ask about therapy again. I'd admit I did it on purpose. I loved TJ and how supportive he was of me talking to a professional about my issues, but I didn't want to rehash all the unwanted emotions that bubbled up to the surface today. I didn't want to admit to him I was unsure and scared about going back.

He stroked my hair as I lay naked in his arms and held onto him. "Baby girl?"

"Yeah, T?" I murmured as I buried my head into his chest. This was exactly what I wanted from him tonight. To be held in his arms while he told me everything would be okay, even though I was cracking at the seams.

"I'm proud of you for going today. Promise me you'll go again?"

He tipped my head up to look at him, and the worry I saw etched across his face almost broke me. I didn't want him to be consumed with worry because of my mental state.

I nodded. "Tristan?"

A smile curled around his lips at his first name coming out of my mouth. "Yeah, baby girl?"

"I just want to be held tonight. I don't want to talk about it."

He gave me that lopsided grin. "Okay, baby. I want that too. Missed you every night when I was away."

I laughed. "Wow. I think I bewitched you. That's not something play boy TJ Desjardins would say."

He grinned. "Yeah, you and that sweet pussy did me in."

I gave him a playful glare. "Stop! That's not it."

He ran a hand down my face and stroked his thumb across my lips. "Or maybe it's this sweet mouth. Or your awesome tits."

I shook my head at his antics, but I knew what he was doing. He was trying to get me to laugh and lighten the mood.

He gave me a quick kiss. "Or maybe it's because you're my better half."

My heart did cartwheels in my chest at the sweet, corny words. Who would have thought I'd ever hear them from this man in particular?

He gave me that naughty grin. "But mostly, it's your fantastic tits."

I playfully slapped his arm, but I laughed, and when he gave me that naughty grin again, I knew everything would be okay. For now.

CHAPTER TWENTY-FIVE

TJ

"Dude, what're you doing?" Benny asked as he caught me looking through the cookbook he kept on the counter.

We got back from practice a little bit ago, and I had big plans for me and Maxine tonight.

"Maxine's coming over for dinner, and I want to make something for her," I explained.

Benny stroked a hand across his beard. "Does she like Mexican food? Most of that stuff is my abuela's recipes, but we could modify it for her."

"Right, I don't know how to cook vegetarian food."

He furrowed his brow. "Maybe we should call Dinah."

We both looked at each other and laughed. Despite coming from a big Italian family, Dinah wasn't much of a cook. When Noah moved in with her, he came to realize that sometimes she ate snacks for dinner because she didn't feel like cooking. I swear, despite their eight-year difference, Noah was the adult in that relationship.

Benny rolled up his sleeves and walked over to the kitchen. He flipped through the book but eyed me from over it. "You seem nervous."

"I've never made dinner for a chick before," I admitted.

Benny shook his head at me. "I do it for your sister all the time."

"That's different. You're whipped."

He punched me.

"Ow! Dick!"

"Do you want help or not, asshole?"

"Help!"

"Hmm, okay..." He stroked his beard while he flipped through a couple pages, and then he put his finger on one. "Let's make tofu sofritas tacos."

I raised an eyebrow at him.

He pulled out a pad of paper and started jotting down a list of ingredients. "Don't worry, I'll help you. What's the occasion?"

"No occasion. It's her second week of going to therapy, and she was a wreck after the first appointment."

"Ah, so you want to cheer her up."

I nodded. "It took a bit of convincing to get her to go. I thought she was going to walk out when I asked."

"Oh. When she had that nightmare and tried to break up with you?"

I rubbed my jaw. "Yeah. That shit was scary. I'm so afraid of..."

"What?"

I groaned. "Did Rox tell you about Natalie?"

He shook his head.

"She told me I was a useless jock and—"

He interrupted me. "Max doesn't think that about you. You're trying to help her."

I sighed. "I know. Sometimes it's really hard, you know?"

"Yeah, I know. I'm dating your sister, who can be a pain in my ass, but I love her, so I always fight for her. You gotta fight for Max even when she makes it difficult and you want to throw in the towel."

I nodded.

I was glad Benny said he fought for Rox because sometimes she made it hard on herself when she lashed out too quickly without thinking first. I could be that way too, but I'd been trying my hardest not to be that way with Max.

Benny smirked at me. "You seem nervous, bro! She'll appreciate that you tried. I'll walk you through everything."

"I'll owe you one."

He gave me a conspiratorial look. "I might pull that favor soon."

"My sister doesn't want to play for the Philadelphia Liberty, huh?"

He groaned. "So stubborn! I'll help you tonight if you talk to her about it. She needs to be out there on the ice with players of her stature. Beer League's fine, but she should play professionally. Even if the money sucks."

I put out my hand. "Deal."

We shook on it, and then Benny dragged me out to the market.

I spent the rest of the afternoon under Benny's careful eye cooking my girlfriend dinner. A few times, he told me I was doing it wrong. I didn't know how he and Rox didn't kill each other when they were cooking together. She liked to be in control in the kitchen, and Benny was micromanaging me.

We were plating everything when there was a knock on the door. I wiped my hands with a hand towel and went to open it. When I opened it, my beautiful girlfriend was standing behind it with a tear-stained face.

"Oh baby," I cooed, and she walked into my arms.

I wrapped my arms around her and held her to my chest. I ran my hands down her back and rubbed it while I let her cry on my shoulder.

She lifted her head after a few seconds and wiped at her eyes. "I'm sorry."

I tilted her chin up and gave her a quick kiss. "Nothing to be sorry about. Tell me about it?"

She shook her head. "No." She cocked her head at the scene in the kitchen and then looked back at me. "Did you make me dinner?"

"Benny helped."

"Thank you, TJ. That was really nice of you."

I took off her coat and hung it up in the hall closet. She slipped off her shoes and left them at the door. She parked herself at the barstool while Benny handed her a plate.

"You want wine, baby?" I asked.

"Please."

I pulled out the bottle of wine I had been saving for her and poured us glasses.

"Goddamnit," Benny swore as he ate his tacos on the other side of Max and stared at his phone.

"What's wrong?" Max asked.

Benny rubbed a hand down his face. "Rox was gonna come over, but now she wants me to go over there. I'm getting tired of this shit."

I handed Max her glass of wine and came around to sit beside her. We shared a concerned look. "Dude, just ask her," I said.

"I want to wait for her lease to be up."

"What are we talking about?" Max interjected.

"Benny wants to ask Rox to move in," I explained.

"Here?" she asked and raised an eyebrow.

Benny shook his head. "No. I want to get a place of our own. I hate being apart all the time. It sucks. I want to cuddle with her every night when I'm not on the road, but half the time, we're trying to figure out whose place we're gonna be at."

"Whipped," I whispered under my breath.

Max slapped my thigh teasingly. "You should talk to her about that," she said to Benny.

He shrugged and ate his tacos at record speed. "I'm out. Don't get up to anything too bad while I'm gone."

I grinned at him. "She likes to keep me in line."

Benny left in a hurry, and I pondered his predicament. I understood what he was getting at. I hated that I didn't get to wake up with Max every morning. Maybe if I had her beside me every day, I wouldn't be afraid of her slipping out of my fingers.

She must have sensed what I was thinking. "TJ, I'm not moving in here."

"Why not?"

She set her taco down and took a sip of her wine. "We're not there yet."

I brought her hand up to my lips and kissed it. "But I love waking up beside you."

Her face softened. "I love that too, but it's too soon. You need to learn to live by yourself."

I felt like she had been talking to my sister. Rox was the only person who called me on not liking being by myself.

"I like when you're with me."

A smile played across her lips. "I like being with you, but we just started dating. It's way too soon to move in together."

"I don't like being alone with my thoughts," I admitted.

Her face softened. "Oh, T. Is that because of Natalie?"

I nodded. "I hate the doubt that creeps in when I'm by myself."

She cupped my face. "You're enough, okay? Don't let that stuff that goes on with me make you feel like you're not. I love you, okay?"

I nodded and gave her a quick kiss before going back to eating.

"Thanks for dinner. It was nice," she said after we finished dinner.

"I know therapy's hard for you, so I wanted to do something nice since I leave tomorrow again. I hate leaving you."

She put her hand on my jaw. "TJ, I know it sucks that you travel a lot, and this hockey girlfriend thing is hard, but this is your job. I get it."

"How are you the best?" I asked her.

She shook her head. "I'm not. I put you through too much."

"You want to talk about it?"

She shook her head, and I watched her down her wine. "That's what the therapy's for. It's too hard."

"I'm here, though. You know that, right?"

She gave me a sad smile. "I know, baby. I love that you want to be supportive, but it's like opening up an old wound each time I talk about it."

I nodded. I guess I understood that. It was hard when I told her about the stuff with Natalie. I know Natalie apologized, but that hurt still lingered with me. It stuck with me.

"I think I need your help," I said.

She cleared away our plates and started loading the dishwasher. "I got it."

"Not with the dishes. You don't have to do that."

"You made dinner. Let me do the cleanup."

I let her take my plate and wineglass and watched her soak the pan we made the tofu in. I liked her in my kitchen, taking care of me. Was that sexist? Maybe, but she looked like she belonged there. I understood now why Noah moved in with Dinah so quickly. Being away from Max was the worst feeling in the world. A part of my heart stayed in Philly while I was gone.

"Benny needs help to convince my sister."

"To move in with him? She'll cave!" she said over the running water.

I got up and walked around to her. I wrapped my arms around her waist and pressed a kiss to her neck. "No. To convince her to play for the Liberty."

She laughed but leaned back to give me more access to her neck. "Oh! I've already tried that. She's stubborn."

"Family trait," I teased.

"Let's talk about your sister later, okay?"

"Hmm, why's that?"

"You know why," she muttered under her breath, but she wouldn't turn around and look at me.

Despite bringing her out of her shell, Max could still be a little shy. She never initiated sex, and sometimes it made me feel like a creep always asking for it. I wanted her to be comfortable with whatever we did. It was why I double-checked when she agreed to that sexy video chat session when I was on the road. She still struggled with her shame about sex, so it was important she told me what she wanted.

"Tell me what you want."

"You know what I want," she grumbled.

I smirked at her and turned her around, capturing her lips in mine. Her hands went into my hair, and I lifted her up onto the counter. Max was such a tiny thing, I sometimes forgot how annoying it was to crane my neck down to kiss her. She wrapped her legs around my waist as we kissed.

I trailed my lips down to her neck again. "I want you to tell me."

"You know," she muttered.

"Say it."

"I want to ride your fucking cock!" she blurted out.

I chuckled into her neck. I lifted my head up and saw her face red at her outburst. "You're so cute when you swear."

She groaned. "BABY!"

"Use your words, Max. I need to hear it."

"I told you!"

I trailed my lips across her neck, licking and sucking on the spot that got her going. I nipped at her earlobe. "Say it, baby girl. Tell me what you need."

"I want to ride you until you're spent. I want to be underneath you. I want you to...to go down on me. Can we go into your bedroom now and stop talking about it?"

I loved when she let go with me in the bedroom, but it was cute that she still got flustered, even when we both knew it was what she wanted.

"Good girl," I cooed at her as I took her into my bedroom and did exactly that.

I loved this woman so much. Having a girlfriend rocked. It just sucked I traveled so much and had to leave her all the time.

CHAPTER TWENTY-SIX

MAXINE

I nervously tapped my foot and watched the text bubbles come up on my phone. I should be working, but my boyfriend was supposed to get back from the road today, and he said he would bring me lunch after he finished practice. I told him not to, but TJ was picking up sweet gestures from his roommate.

It still amazed me that TJ Desjardins, the guy who asked for my number and never called, ended up being such a caring partner. He might appear like the loud party boy, but deep down, he had a soft gooey center.

He had been great with me these past couple of weeks while I started therapy and worked through my issues. It made him happy I was trying, and it was nice to know I could lean on him when I had a bad session. I noticed the nightmares had lessened since I started talking with my therapist about the things I locked away inside. TJ had been right to push me to talk to a professional, even though I didn't want to admit it.

A loud clearing of a throat startled me, and I almost dropped my phone.

I cringed when I turned and saw Quinn Wellson standing in front of my cube. Not only was she my boss's boss but also the GM's wife. And she caught me slacking off on the job. A job I freaking hated, but not something you wanted to happen at work. I slid my phone to the other end of my desk.

"Hi! Um, what can I do for you?" I asked and fumbled with my words.

She squeezed my shoulder. "Relax, honey. Can I see you in my office?"

Panic coursed through me at those words. What could she possibly want to see me in her office for? If I was getting fired, wouldn't Rox be with her too? My hands got sweaty, and I wiped them on my pants while my heart beat loudly in my chest. I knew I couldn't actually hear it in my head; it was just a symptom of the silent anxiety attack.

Crap, I didn't need this today.

"Is now okay?" Quinn asked.

I swallowed thickly and tried to focus on my breathing.

"Sure," I choked out.

I got up from my desk and followed her to her office down the hall. I swore all eyes were on me, but I couldn't tell if that was just my imagination. My heartbeat sounded louder, and it distracted me so much I hadn't realized I missed the question Quinn asked me. I didn't even remember sitting in the chair across from her desk.

Crap, this was bad.

"I'm sorry, what?" I asked.

"Debra, the social media manager, is going on maternity leave. I asked Rox if you could help, and she thought you'd be a good fit."

"She agreed?" I asked. Rox said nothing to me about this.

"Look, I'll be honest with you. Before I hired Rox, I wanted to give you her job. I asked you twice for a reason, but Rox mentioned she thinks you don't particularly like your job. I have to admit that's disappointing..."

I froze at her words and stopped listening to the rest of her sentence.

I never told Rox how much I hated my job. I loved working for the team, but I hated the work itself. Was I going to get fired because I didn't like my job? Rox could tell?

Then a dark thought emerged in the back of my mind. TJ knew I didn't like my job. I had mentioned I wasn't passionate about it and didn't like it when we went to the speakeasy. He and his sister were close, so if my boss knew I hated my job, there was only one person who could have told her.

My palms were sweaty, and I felt like I couldn't breathe.

"Maxine, are you okay?" Quinn asked, and I realized I hadn't answered her last couple of questions.

"Uh-huh," I lied.

I was not okay. A hot flash of anger ran through me at the thought TJ had jeopardized my career. I couldn't believe he did this to me. I had trusted him. I opened up myself to him, let all my walls down, and then he told his sister I didn't like my job. What right did he have to tell her that?

"Rox didn't tell you any of this, did she?" Quinn asked.

I shook my head.

"Shit. I thought she talked to you about this. I didn't want to spring this on you without warning. It's gonna be a lot of extra work."

"It's okay," I lied.

She gave me a sympathetic smile. "Talk to Rox about it, and we'll figure out a plan."

"Okay, sure. I gotta get back to it," I mumbled.

"Thanks, Max!"

I went back to my cubicle with my mind spinning. My head swam with all the thoughts in my head that I didn't hear the voice calling my name until muscular arms were holding onto my shoulders.

"What's wrong?" TJ asked. Confusion swirled inside his hazel eyes.

"Did you tell your sister I hated my job?" I snapped at him.

He looked taken aback at the venom in my voice. "Did I what?"

"Did you tell her I hate it here?" I hissed.

He held up the takeout bag from the vegan fast-food place I loved. "How about we go eat lunch and talk about what's bothering you?"

White-hot rage coursed through me, and I shot him a glare. "It's not gonna matter if I'm about to get fired because of you!"

A dark shadow of hurt fell across his face, and I immediately knew I had overreacted. He wouldn't have looked that wounded if he had done what I thought he did. Then his face transformed into a neutral mask, and I knew I messed up.

I sighed. "T, I'm..."

He balled his hands into fists. "You know what? Call me later."

"TJ," I tried again, pleading with him to let me apologize.

He wouldn't even look at me. Instead, he stared down at

his shoes. I shouldn't have lashed out at him like that or accused him of something like that. I should have waited to talk to his twin sister, but I was angry and in the middle of another panic attack, and I wasn't thinking straight.

His eyes were a storm of torment and anguish when he finally looked up at me. It was the same look he had on his face the night he begged me to go to therapy.

I was the worst girlfriend in the entire world.

"I'm gonna go," he muttered.

"You travel tomorrow."

He was bringing me lunch today because he had another road stretch, and we wouldn't see each other for a couple of days. Doing lunches together was a way we snuck in time together during his busy schedule.

"Yeah, well, maybe I need *my* space," he snapped at me.

I reared back at that reaction. "What?"

He ran his hand down his jaw, and he looked like he regretted lashing out, but neither of us could take back what we had said. "Maybe you were right to let me down easily. Maybe this isn't gonna work out."

"What are you saying?" I asked and bit my lip to keep it from quivering.

Was he really breaking up with me? I didn't blame him—I hadn't been fair to him—but he wasn't giving me the chance to apologize.

"We'll talk when I get back," he said firmly.

I didn't bother stopping him, and he didn't look back as he stormed out.

I was pretty sure that meant we were done, and I deserved it. I shouldn't have freaked out on him. I should have talked to Rox. Instead, I let my insecurities get the best of me like I always did. I didn't deserve the love TJ had been willing to give to me. I pushed him away at every turn.

Maybe today was the last straw. My accusation made him finally snap and realize we were better off apart. *He* was better off without me.

I still burst into tears as soon as he stormed out. We were doomed to fail from the start, but I knew our ending was completely my fault. I pushed him away one last time, and a broken heart was just the consequence of my own immature actions.

CHAPTER TWENTY-SEVEN

TJ

I was pretty sure Max and I were over, and it was totally my fault. I didn't know why she thought I was the reason she was getting fired, but storming out wasn't my best moment. I was kicking myself for telling her we wouldn't work out, but I couldn't take it back now. Something was up with her, but rather than ask her what was bothering her, I let my hurt get the better of me. I felt like an asshole.

This was why I never did relationships. I wasn't built for this shit.

"Dude. I asked you the same question three times. What gives?" Noah asked as he punched me in the arm.

After I left the arena offices, I asked Noah to hang. Noah, being the sensitive guy he was, knew something was up, but instead of asking, he threw a game controller at me.

I didn't have a chance to answer because Dinah came home from work and distracted Noah. He got up, and I watched as he lifted her up into his arms so he could kiss her. The tiny woman laughed as she kissed him back.

I rubbed at my chest as if my heart was physically aching because I already missed that with Max. I shouldn't have been such an asshole today.

"Babe, put me down," Dinah said to Noah.

He obliged and helped her out of her coat. Watching them together was kind of sweet.

Dinah sat down on the couch next to me. "Honey, what's wrong?" she asked.

Good ole, D. She always knew when I needed an ear to listen.

"I fucked up," I said.

"With Max?" she asked.

Noah shuffled into the kitchen. When he came back into the living room, he handed me a beer before sitting down next to Dinah. "Figured that's what this was about."

"What happened?" Dinah asked.

I scrubbed a hand across my jaw and sighed. "I don't know. She was in a bad mood when I went over there to meet her for lunch, and then she accused me of telling Roxie she hated her job. She thought she was gonna get fired, and it was my fault."

Dinah pursed her lips. "Okay...how did *you* fuck up, then? It sounds like she was the one being the asshole."

I groaned.

"Bud, what did you say?" Noah asked.

"I told her I needed space."

Noah groaned. "Bud!"

"It gets worse," I warned.

"T, what did you say?" Dinah asked.

"I think I broke up with her."

She punched me in the arm. "Why did you do that?"

I rubbed my arm. "Ow! How come all the women in my life punch harder than hockey players?"

She smirked. "Three older brothers!"

I groaned and leaned my head on the back of the couch. "I fucked up really bad. Maybe I've always been right."

"About what?" Dinah asked.

"I'm not the relationship type. She's been constantly pushing me away and telling me I'm not good enough."

Dinah narrowed her eyes at me, but Noah spoke up instead. "When has Max ever said that? Because based on our previous conversations, it's her who thinks she doesn't deserve you."

"She hasn't," I grumbled. "But I know she's thinking about it. She says I don't deserve her and that she's this burden. It's so hard sometimes with her, but I love her and want her to be happy."

"But you don't think she'll be happy with you?" Noah asked and stroked his beard.

"Why would she? I'm a fuckup."

"Oh, honey..." Dinah sighed.

Noah stared at me for a long time, and then he looked at his girlfriend for reassurance. "Are you confused? Because I'm confused."

The tiny brunette nodded. "Yeah. It sounds like you're talking about something else, not about the fight you got in with Max."

A lot of what I was feeling wasn't about anything Max said today. It was all shit Natalie said to me in high school. When Max lashed out at me, saying I was going to get her fired, I projected all the darkness I kept inside on her. I was a Grade A asshole. My girlfriend had clearly been upset and probably in the middle of a panic attack, and instead of talking her through it like I always promised, I stormed off like a petulant child.

I watched my friends share a concerned look, and then Dinah got up. "Stay for dinner, T?"

"Nah, I'm good."

"My cooking isn't that bad!" she teased as she walked into their kitchen.

"Apologize," Noah urged me.

He was right, but I wasn't sure an apology would cut it. Max looked crushed before I stormed out. I promised I'd never hurt her, but then I went and did it today. I looked at my phone but ignored all the texts from my sister. I swiped over to Max's name on my contact list.

ME: *Baby girl, I'm sorry. I was an asshole.*

I saw the text bubbles pop up on my screen, showing that she was typing something back. They stopped and restarted a few times before a text popped up on my screen.

BABY GIRL: *K.*

"In person!" Noah said and shook his head at me. "Lovey!" he called into the kitchen.

"What?" Dinah called back.

"TJ's hopeless!"

She walked back into the living room and gave him a quick kiss. They were a little too cutesy for me right now. I needed to get out of here.

"I'm gonna go."

"You sure?" Noah asked.

"I need to be alone," I said.

Dinah frowned. "Have dinner with us, and then you can go grovel, okay?"

I shook my head. "I'm good. Thanks for listening to me."

I didn't let either of them get another word in edgewise,

and I went next door. Benny left me a note about leftovers in the fridge, so I ate that in silence in front of the blank TV screen. Dinah and Noah tried to help, but I think I was beyond that. I fucked up too big, and I wasn't sure I had a girlfriend anymore.

I wondered if Max was going to close her heart off from me forever now. I should have gone to her and apologized in person and talked it through with her. Her accusations hurt me. I never told my sister that my girlfriend didn't like her job; that wasn't my place, and it bothered me that Max immediately jumped to that conclusion. I didn't want to lose her, but my reaction today made me feel like I already had.

I had to use this next road trip to think about what I really wanted.

❄

When we touched down in Toronto, I got a text from my dad asking to meet me for a drink after I got through all the team bullshit today. We didn't play until tomorrow, so I knew my sister called him.

I tried to compose another text to Maxine. I wanted to call her, but that 'K' text had seared into my brain and told me everything I needed to know. I knew I'd messed up, but I wasn't sure how to fix it. I also knew it wasn't my fault alone, but I couldn't help but feel like such a fuckup.

I wasn't in the mood to talk to my dad before the game. To Alain Desjardins, hockey was everything. I had a feeling he would tell me to focus on winning the cup instead of my broken heart.

It was hard to have a hockey player as a dad. I was constantly compared to him and expected to play as well as him. They expected me to be a faster skater, a better goal scorer, and a smarter playmaker. I was doing my best, but I would never shake the feeling that my best wasn't good enough. That *I* wasn't good enough.

When I met my dad at the bar, I was thankful there was already a beer waiting for me, and I took a huge gulp of it.

"Buddy," Dad said.

"I think I fucked up," I blurted out.

Dad raised an eyebrow and raked a hand through his greying hair. "Yeah, your sister told me you're having girlfriend troubles. I didn't even know you had a girlfriend."

"We've been dating for a couple months," I said.

I let my sentence hang in the air for a moment. Dad picked up his beer and sipped it like he was waiting for me to continue. I stared into my beer glass, not sure where to start.

I took my phone out and showed him my background. It was a photo Rox had taken of Max and me at my condo when we had people over for a party. In the photo, I was standing behind Max with my arms wrapped around her while she looked up at me and smiled.

He slid the phone back to me. "She's cute. Tell me about her."

"She's shy until you get to know her. She's a vegetarian, and she loves the Bulldogs, and Claude LaVoie was her childhood crush."

Dad chuckled at that last part, but I ignored him and continued.

"But she was in a car accident in high school that killed her parents, and now she has night terrors and anxiety. I was such an asshole to her when she was having a bad day."

"You apologize?"

I nodded.

"What did she say?"

I shook my head. "All she texted back was 'k.' Like, what the fuck?"

Dad furrowed his brow and held up his hand at me. "Wait a second. You apologized via text message?"

"Yeah?"

He glared at me. "Are you serious?"

"What?"

He pinched the bridge of his nose between his thumb and finger. "Goddamnit, kid. You apologize in *person*. How are you that thick? You love this woman?"

"I pushed her away and told her I didn't think it was going to work out."

Dad sighed. "What was the fight even about?"

I shrugged. "She thinks I told Roxie she hates her job."

He furrowed his brow. "What does your sister have to do with it?"

I sighed. "Roxie's her boss."

"Christ, kid," Dad swore with the shake of his head. "Why would that lead to you saying you don't think it's gonna work out?"

"Because I once again proved to her I'm not good enough."

He held up his hand for me to stop. "I'm sorry, what? You're not good enough for her? Did she say that?"

I rubbed the back of my neck nervously. "No. Nat did."

Dad rolled his eyes so hard I thought he might go cross-eyed. "Jesus fucking Christ. Tristan, I want you to be happy, but thinking you don't deserve happiness because of something a troubled sixteen-year-old said to you is the stupidest thing I've heard. When you get home, you better grovel your fucking ass off."

I gave him a sideways glance. "You sound like you have experience with that."

He gulped down the rest of his beer. "You think everything's perfect with your mother?"

"Well yeah, you do anything she says."

He tipped back his head and laughed. "Tristan, we almost got a divorce."

"What? When?"

My parents seemed so solid. To the point, it was embarrassing as a kid to watch your parents kiss.

"I didn't want to retire," he said with a frown.

Oh, shit.

I vaguely remembered them fighting a lot about that. Dad retired because of one too many hits to the head and concussion complications. Back then, the league wasn't doing enough to combat the rampant head injuries. Some people would argue they still weren't doing enough about it.

"What did you do?" I asked.

"Well, my last scan was terrible. They found spots on my brain."

"Like LaVoie."

Dad nodded. "But I was trying to be that tough hockey guy. Your mom was scared of losing me. We fought about it a lot."

"But you quit anyway. Why?"

He sighed. "Tristan, I love your mother. She's the light of my life. She packed a bag and took you and your sister to your gran's."

Shit. I had a vague memory of being at Gran's house without Dad, but Mom wouldn't tell us why.

"How did you fix it?"

"I quit that night. Hockey was my career, but your

mother and you kids were my life. Also groveling and lots of flowers."

"Okay..."

He sighed. "Then your sister came out."

When my twin came out, our mom told her 'bisexuality didn't exist.' Rox and my parents hadn't spoken in years because of it. Last summer, she finally agreed to talk to them again. Mostly because Dad showed up in Philly on our birthday.

"But Rox and Mom are trying to fix things now."

Dad nodded. "Yeah, but it was hard on our marriage. Your mother doesn't get bisexuality. I don't either, but if Roxie's happy, I'm happy for her. It took your mother a long time to realize that. That was a hard couple of years for us."

I glared at him. "It was hard for Roxie too!"

Dad ran a frustrated hand down his face. "Bud, I know. We were both wrong, but I'm just saying I know a little about groveling and knowing when you fucked up. When you get back to Philly, what are you gonna do?"

"Grovel and bring her flowers?" I asked.

"And apologize to her face."

I frowned. "I really messed up."

"You love her?"

I nodded. "I do. I've never felt this way about someone before."

"Not even Nat?"

I shook my head. "Not even Nat. I've never let someone in before, but I'm afraid I can't fix it."

"If you want it to work, you'll fight for her."

I took a swig of my beer and nodded.

Dad looked pointedly at me. "Can we talk about how shit you are on the power play now?"

I groaned and downed the rest of my beer. "Is that the real reason you wanted me to meet you for a beer?"

He laughed and shrugged.

"Dad!"

"Nah, Roxie told me you needed to talk but you wouldn't say anything unless I pushed you. But yeah, your special teams looks weak."

I rolled my eyes but took another sip of my drink as we started talking shop. We ordered another round, but I didn't stay for long because I would get my ass handed to me by Coach if I missed curfew.

When I got back to my hotel room, my hand lingered on my phone. Against my better judgment, I texted Max.

ME: *I'm sorry.*

BABY GIRL: *K*

ME: *Can we talk when I get home?*

BABY GIRL: *I guess.*

I groaned and put my phone down on the bedside table. Groveling it was...but first, I had to win these next two games.

CHAPTER TWENTY-EIGHT

MAXINE

J was supposed to get back from his latest road trip today, but I wasn't sure I wanted to see him. I had been such a bitch the last time I saw him. When he said he needed space and suggested we break up, I knew it was over between us. I didn't deserve the love he tried to give me. It didn't surprise me he finally came to his senses.

He texted me exactly once while he was on the road, only to ask if we could talk when he got home. That meant only one thing; he wanted to break up. We were just delaying the inevitable because of his travel schedule. I half wished he would have done it over text, so I wouldn't have to look into the face of the man I loved as he ripped my heart from my chest.

"Doesn't your man get back today?" Keiana asked, startling me from my daydreaming on the couch.

"I guess."

She raised an eyebrow. "You guess?"

"I think we broke up."

"Since when?" she screeched. "What happened? Why didn't you tell me?"

I shrugged. "Doesn't matter."

She looked at her watch. "Wait, shouldn't you be at work?"

"Took a sick day."

She narrowed her dark eyes at me. "Is that because you're avoiding TJ?"

Well, no, I took off because I was avoiding his sister. I still wasn't sure if I was getting fired or not. I had been keeping busy getting up to speed on the social media stuff that I wasn't at my desk all week. Rox wanted to get something on the calendar to discuss my workload, but I was sure she would still fire me, so I called out sick.

I didn't have to answer my bestie because the doorbell rang instead. Keiana went to go see who was at the door. When she walked back into the living room, Rox was following her and carrying a bouquet of tiger lilies.

"Okay, two things," Rox began. She walked over to the coffee table and set down the flowers. "One, these are from my brother, but he had practice. And, two...we need to talk."

I sat up on the couch. "Can't you wait until tomorrow to fire me?"

She sat next to me on the couch and rubbed the bridge of her nose. I noticed Kei casually slipped away. She didn't like drama.

"Maxine, why do you think I'm gonna fire you?"

"Because Quinn said you knew I didn't like my job."

She sighed. "Um, that's not a secret. You aren't exactly enthusiastic about it."

Oh.

Oh, crap. I was such an asshole. I blew up at TJ because

I thought he told his sister how much I hated working in sales. Did everyone know I hated it?

"Oh. So why did you tell Quinn I should help with Debra's maternity leave?" I asked.

She pinned me with an annoyed look. "Why would you think that meant you were getting fired? How does that even make sense?"

Okay, she got me there. I don't think I was in the right frame of mind when I talked to Quinn.

She reached down into her briefcase and pulled out a print-out from the team's website. She shoved it at me. "I think you need to move to marketing."

"What?" I asked.

I scanned across the paper and saw it was a job listing for a social media coordinator. At the bottom, scrawled in Rox's handwriting, were the words, 'PERFECT FOR MAX!' in all caps.

She steepled her hands. "You aren't happy in sales. But I also know you'll never leave because you love working for the team. I put a good word in for you, and it's why Quinn wanted your help instead of outsourcing."

"Why?" I asked.

"When the marketing department was short-staffed and asked for help with a game day event, Debra said you were a great asset. It impressed her when you gave her some off-the-cuff ideas for content for our channels. Like the podcast! I know that was your idea."

"The WAG podcast?"

"Yes! And it's brought in a lot of female fans. That was your idea."

I waved her off. "I gave her the idea. She took it and ran with it."

"You're more suited for that sort of thing. You don't

belong in sales. It's why I told Quinn to ask for your help, because you're capable at any job, even if you don't like it."

"Oh."

She rolled her eyes. "Yeah, oh! I wanted to talk to you before Quinn did. I like you a lot, Max. I don't want to lose you as a team member, but I can't watch a member of my team be unhappy."

"You really think I should apply for this job?"

"Yes, that's why I'm here. Because I know you're not sick, and you're avoiding me and my brother."

I sighed. "We're done. He doesn't have to say anything else to me."

She groaned. "Oh my God, you're both so frustrating!"

I gave her a quizzical look.

"Max, my brother thinks he's the one who fucked up. Relationships are a give and take. You think Benny and I still don't fight?"

I shook my head. "No way. You're like the 'it' couple."

She barked out a laugh. "Definitely not. We still fight, but now I get to ride his dick after it's over. Tristan's really trying, Max. I swear, you two are such a pair."

"What do you mean?"

"You keep pushing my brother away because you don't want to burden him. But when you do that, it brings up old shit for him. Makes him feel like he's not good enough for you."

"Natalie," I spit out.

She nodded. "Don't get me wrong—I love Nat. She was there for me when my ex kicked me out...but she was horrible to my brother in high school. I don't think that pain ever left him."

"I don't want him to feel that way. He apologized via

text, and I was so passive-aggressive, all I wrote back was 'k'!"

Her shoulders shook with a laugh. "I know. It was supremely passive-aggressive. I'm kind of impressed."

I groaned and put my head in my hands. "Rox, I think we're done. I think he broke up with me."

"You two are so annoying! He wouldn't have apologized and wanted to talk if he wanted to break up. And he wouldn't have asked me to bring you flowers."

I wrung my hands in my lap. Maybe it was just a dumb fight over a misunderstanding. Instead of being grown-ups about it, we both said things we regretted. We needed to talk it out and apologize. TJ was really trying. God, I swear he was a saint to deal with all my stuff. How many times did I try to break up with him because of my issues? Did it all start with that first night we went home together and I tried to ghost him? TJ was persistent in chasing me, but if I kept pushing him away, one day, he wouldn't come back.

I swiped at my eyes again. And gave Rox a muttered 'thanks' when she handed me the box of tissues off the coffee table. I blotted my eyes.

"You okay?" she asked.

I shook my head. "I miss him."

"He missed you, too. He's been a wreck."

"Yeah, he's been playing like hot garbage," I blurted and then cringed.

The curvy woman beside me laughed. "You're not wrong."

"Rox, I really messed up. I accused him of getting me fired and didn't even let him defend himself! How can I get him to take me back?"

"He's a man. Get on your knees!" Keiana called from the kitchen.

Rox laughed. "Oh my God, I like this girl."

Keiana came back into the living room and took a seat in the armchair.

I glared at her. "You two aren't helpful!"

I reached down and fingered a petal on one of the flowers. I loved that TJ remembered my favorite flowers after a random conversation. He had been so thoughtful.

I saw a card attached, and I opened it up. Inside was a note scrawled in his terrible handwriting, and my heart ached at the fact I caused him so much pain.

Baby girl.

I'm sorry. Let's talk. I don't want to break up. I love you more than hockey.

Love,

TJ

"Geez, what did you do to my emotionless brother?" Rox asked as she read over my shoulder.

"Rox, I don't know what to do!"

"Make him dinner. He likes when you baby him," Keiana suggested.

Rox nodded her head. "Yes, do that! That's how Benny got me to stop hating him."

Keiana laughed. "That man's fine. How did you ever hate him?"

"He asked if my tits were fake!" Rox exclaimed. "Also, I'm an asshole."

Keiana laughed. "Okay, I need the full story there."

Rox waved her off. "Later. We need to make sure these fools work it out."

Keiana nodded in agreement.

I chewed on my lips. "Okay...but I feel like dinner's not enough. I need to make a big grand gesture."

Keiana made a universal sign for blow jobs with her tongue in her cheek, which made Rox laugh.

"You both are jerks!" I said.

"She's not wrong. You gotta wine and dine and sixty-nine him!" Rox joked.

"The worst, both of you!" I huffed.

Rox cackled. "I gotta jet anyway."

"Are you mad at me for calling out sick?"

"Yeah, but I knew you were going through some shit." Rox got up from the couch and took her briefcase with her. "We'll talk tomorrow, but seriously, if you're helping while Debra's on maternity leave, you will be perfect to work on her team. I don't want someone on my team who hates what they do."

I nodded. "I should have talked to you before lashing out at TJ."

She gave me a smug look. "Yeah, that's some Roxanne Desjardins asshole behavior. Unusual for you, though."

"I was having a panic attack. I wasn't in a good place."

"I get that, but you need to grovel. My brother's distraught. I don't think he's ever felt for anyone what he feels for you. He thinks he's messed everything up. You two need to work through it together."

"Thanks, Rox."

I stared down at the flowers in front of me as she left, and I pulled out my phone to shoot TJ a message.

ME: *Let's talk. My place. I'll make dinner.*

TJ: *K!*

"What are you gonna do?" Keiana asked.

"Make him that lasagna he likes. Grovel a lot. I don't know, Kei."

She pointed to the flowers. "It seems like he messed up too, and he knows it. It's good he has his sister in his corner."

I nodded. "Sometimes it's like dating both of them. Good thing I actually like Rox."

"You want help today? I have plans, but you know I'll cancel for you."

I shook my head. "Nah. I got this. Thanks, Kei."

She gave me a hug. "Love you, Max. You know I'm always here for you. I think you need to fix this with your man, though. He's the only person who has ever gotten you out of your shell."

"What if he doesn't want me back? What if he changed his mind after he had time to think about it?"

She shook her head. "Nah, you're hopelessly in love. Apologize and then get it in."

"Keiana!"

She laughed. "You know I'm right. Love you, hun. Now get to work on winning back your man."

I shook my head at her, but I was glad Kei would always be in my corner.

CHAPTER TWENTY-NINE

TJ

For the fifth time, I ran my hand through my hair and stared at my reflection in my bathroom mirror. I splashed the aftershave Max liked on my face and realized I was nervous. I might have been a dick to her when she texted today asking to talk. I hoped she didn't want to break up. After talking with my dad in Toronto and being away from her for a couple of days, I knew what I wanted.

"Bro, you look fine!" Benny said as he leaned against the doorway of my bedroom with my sister at his side.

Rox came into my room and stood in front of me. "What are you gonna wear?" she asked.

I gestured down the length of my body to the button-down plaid shirt and dark wash jeans I was already wearing. "What's wrong with this?"

"Nothing. You look fine," Benny said. He gave my sister a stern look. "Angel, he's fine."

My sister bit her lip but nodded. To me, she said, "I

want both of you to be happy. Don't give up because of one fight."

"Angel, it's not your relationship," Benny tried again.

She gave him the finger, and I smiled at how some things never changed.

"Benny, shut it! I'm talking to my brother."

He rolled his eyes and walked out of the room. He knew when to pick his battles with her.

Rox smoothed down an invisible wrinkle on my shirt. "Be honest with her and tell her how hurt you were. But you also have to apologize for being in the wrong, too."

I batted her hand away. "*You're* telling *me* to apologize? That's rich."

"I know I'm a bitch, but I know when to say sorry."

"ANGEL!" Benny yelled from the kitchen. "What did I say about calling yourself a bitch?"

"Oooh, you're in trouble," I teased and pinched her side.

She punched my arm. "Dick. He gets so mad when I call myself that."

"Because he loves you and doesn't see you that way."

She shrugged. "I don't know why not. I was mean to him for years."

"Is that why you're so invested in my failed relationship?"

She frowned. "Tristan, it's not failed, not yet. Max feels awful. She knows she messed up too."

"I better go."

"Good luck!"

I went down to the parking garage and got into my Maserati. I drove across town to South Philly with my nerves in overdrive. After finding a parking spot a couple blocks from Maxine's house, I sat in my car and tried to work up the courage to go inside.

I wasn't sure what to expect from dinner tonight. If she wanted to break up, she wouldn't have cooked me dinner first. It didn't stop the nerves from swirling around in the pit of my stomach. I couldn't help the ache I felt in my chest when I thought of life without Max. She wormed her way inside my heart, and I didn't want to let her go. A few days without her had felt dreary, like a storm cloud had been hovering above my head.

I grabbed the bottle of wine off the passenger seat and got out of my car. I stood on her doorstep waiting for her to answer and half wondered if she was gonna let me in at all.

She opened the door and gave me a half-hearted smile. She looked comfy in a pair of leggings that hugged her ass and an oversized sweater. I liked when she dressed relaxed like this. I liked her in sexy outfits, too. Or nothing.

Focus, Desjardins!

"Can I come in?" I asked after we stood there staring at each for a moment too long.

"Oh yeah, sorry. Come in," she said, but she looked flustered. I handed her the bottle of wine, which she sprinted away with as I took my shoes and coat off.

It smelled amazing in her house, and I recognized the scent of the lasagna she always made for me.

I walked into the kitchen and watched her pull the dish of lasagna out of the oven. She had already set the table and poured wine for both of us. I smiled when I saw the tiger lillies in the center of the table. I was glad my sister could deliver them for me.

I was physically aching to kiss her, to pull her into my arms, and beg for her forgiveness. Max walked over to the table and set the lasagna down.

"Thanks for the flowers," she said before she sat down, and we started on the salad.

I didn't know what to say, so I ate my food and sipped on my wine in silence.

This was so uncomfortable. I didn't want us to break up, but I didn't know how to fix the rift between us.

Silently we finished our salads, and each took big helpings of the lasagna. She said it wasn't anything special, but it tasted so good.

"Is it okay?" she asked.

"What?"

She gestured to my plate. "Dinner."

I furrowed my brow at her and swallowed more of the lasagna. She put a lot of care into dinner tonight like she always did. Max was fantastic in the kitchen, and it showed. She was definitely trying to impress me tonight. Her cooking was awesome, but I'd have to run an extra mile or two tomorrow.

"Yeah. It's amazing, like everything you cook."

She frowned. "Oh."

"What's wrong?"

She looked at me with her big blue eyes shiny with tears, and I felt like a dick. "You look so mad at me, and I know I deserve it."

I put my fork down and pushed my chair out from under the table. "C'mere."

"What?"

I gestured for her to come over to me. She took a big sip of her wine and then walked over to me. I pulled her into my lap, cradling her against my chest. I felt her salty tears against my neck, and it made me feel like even more of a dick.

I lifted her chin up so she would look at me. "Oh, baby girl," I cooed as I cupped her face and wiped away the tears.

"I'm sorry," she blubbered. "I messed everything up."

"S'okay, baby. I'm sorry too."

"No, it's not! I was horrible to you. I was having a panic attack, and I took my feelings out on you. I should have talked to you instead of accusing you of costing me my job."

"You were having another panic attack that day?" I asked.

I knew she wasn't okay the day we had that fight, but her accusations hurt me too much, and I hadn't been thinking straight. I wished I hadn't told her we weren't a good idea. I wished I hadn't been so immature that I stormed out instead of talking it through with her.

She nodded. "I thought I was gonna get fired."

"Why?"

She groaned. "I should have talked to your sister first. Rox's boss, Quinn, pulled me into her office about helping the social media team while the manager was on maternity leave. Then she said she knew I hated my job, and all I could think about was that they were going to fire me."

I furrowed my brow. "I don't understand what that has to do with me."

She frowned. "I jumped to the conclusion that you told Rox. That wasn't fair of me. Or even rational."

"I didn't tell Roxie that. That's your business."

She nodded. "I know that *now*. Rox came over today and told me she wants me to apply for a job opening on the social media team."

"Baby, that's great! Roxie wouldn't want you to move somewhere else if she was going to fire you."

She grimaced. "I know. I wasn't thinking straight that day and took it out on you. That wasn't right. I'm sorry."

"I'm sorry too."

"For what? I was the jerkface."

I caressed her face. "No, baby, I was too. I shouldn't

have said we weren't a good idea. I was hurt, and I took it out on you. I shouldn't have stormed out, either."

She laced her hands together behind my head. "You still want me?"

I leaned forward and pressed my lips to hers. Kissing her was like coming home. It had only been a couple of days, but I missed this. It was totally karma or the hockey gods' way of getting back at me for chirping my teammates for being too 'whipped.'

I got why Noah or Riley always had that dopey look on their faces when they saw their women. I got why Benny stopped talking to anyone when my sister walked into the room. That was Max for me. Everything else faded away when she was near. Those few days without her when I didn't know where we stood had been bleak.

I pulled away before she could kiss me back. I cradled her face in my hands and looked into her eyes. "Maxine, you drown out the darkness inside me. You're my other half, my better half."

"T, I'm not any of that stuff."

"You are, and so much more. I like the way you take care of me. Like when you bring me an ice pack without me having to ask when I've taken too many hits into the boards. I love that you get along with my sister, and you keep me in line. You make me feel like maybe I deserve love. Even on those days when I feel like such a fuckup."

"You deserve love, but maybe with someone a little less broken."

"If you're broken, so am I, and we can fix our broken pieces together to become whole."

She squinted at me. "Are you making a sex joke?"

I barked out a laugh. "No, but..." I waggled my

eyebrows at her, and she finally broke out in laughter. The sound of that was angelic music to my ears.

"Such a perv!"

I gave her my lopsided grin. "Your perv."

"TJ, I don't know if I can be a good girlfriend to you. I feel like I messed up so much already."

"You messed up, but so did I. We might both mess up again, but what's important is that I don't want this to end."

She looked nervous, like she didn't quite believe me. "I don't want us to end either."

"Then stop making me chase you. Let me love you and be loved by you."

"We're both bad at this relationship thing, huh?" she asked as she stroked her hand across my freshly shaved jaw.

I held up my thumb and forefinger. "Maybe a little, but I want to try. Being without you...the world felt dark."

She stopped stroking my jaw and threaded her hands through my hair. "I didn't realize how much I loved you until I thought you were gone. I don't want to feel like that again."

"Then kiss me already and say you're still my girl."

She laughed but closed her eyes and pressed her lips to mine.

CHAPTER THIRTY

MAXINE

I yelped as TJ came up behind me and slid his arms around my waist. "Let me help clean up," he whispered in my ear. The way he kissed my neck told me it was the last thing he wanted to do.

He kissed the slope of my neck, and I bit back a moan.

"Baby, let me clean up," I said but not convincingly. Especially when he slid his hands up the inside of my sweater.

"These leggings should be illegal," he growled into my ear and continued kissing me while his hands roamed up higher.

"Why?"

"Because they make your ass look amazing."

I giggled and tried to push him away, but he spun me around and lifted me up onto the counter. We kissed as if we had been apart for years, not mere days. He framed my face with his hands while he consumed me with his kisses, devouring me like he needed me to breathe. Our fight had barely lasted a week, but the uncertainty in our relationship had been hell. I wasn't sure why he was giving me a second chance, but I wanted him to know how much he meant to me.

"T..." I moaned as his thumb brushed against my nipple.

"Yes, no bra."

"You hate bras."

"Boob prisons," he said as he stroked my nipple in a slow circle. I arched my back to push more of my breast into his hand. "I need you, Maxine."

I wrapped my legs around his waist and yanked his head back up to my face. "Then let's go upstairs, silly!"

He gave me that grin that made my panties melt before he lifted me off the counter and took me up to my room. Once in my bedroom, he dropped me gently on the bed while I laid back and watched him unbutton his plaid shirt. I sat up when I noticed how gingerly he took it off.

"TJ?"

"Hmm?" he responded, but it was muffled by him removing the t-shirt underneath as well. I gasped when I saw the black and blue bruises on his side.

I got off the bed and walked over to him. I knelt down on my knees to get a better look and pressed a finger above the mark. "Baby...that looks so bad. You want to ice it?"

He looked down at me with heat in his eyes. "Are you serious? You're on your knees in front of me, and you're asking if I want to ice my hockey injury?"

I nodded. "It looks bad. I know it's normal to get banged up with your job, but I want to take care of you."

"I want you to take care of me, that's for sure."

I grinned up at him and rubbed my hand on the crouch of his jeans. He felt hard in the kitchen, but now he was even harder. If that was possible. I pressed a gentle kiss to his bruises.

"If you want to kiss my injuries better, I got something else that feels more injured."

I shook my head at his pervy joke and undid the button of his jeans, slowly sliding the zipper down. "Oh yeah, where? Show me?"

He groaned, but I slid his boxers down his thick thighs and released his cock. I licked my lips while I stroked my hand up and down his hard length.

"This?" I asked playfully as I increased the speed of my strokes.

"Max," he moaned and tipped back his head.

"What? You want me to kiss it better?" I joked.

"Baby..."

I glanced up at him. "Hmm?"

"Please," he begged.

"Please, what?" I teased and slid my hand up and down his length.

He reached a hand down and rubbed a thumb across my bottom lip. "Make use of this sweet mouth."

I grinned at him. "Okay!"

I took him in my mouth and enjoyed the taste of him on my lips. I swirled my tongue around the head of his cock and looked up to see his lips parted in ecstasy. I loved seeing that look on his face while I pleasured him.

I took him inside until I felt his cock hit the back of my throat, and then I pulled back. I slid him in and out of my mouth, loving the feeling of doing this for him, until he gripped my hair and pulled me off.

"Be a good girl and get on the bed," he growled.

"You don't want to come in my mouth?"

"Take your clothes off and get your ass in that bed," he ordered.

I bit back a moan and felt heat pool between my legs. I loved when he got all growly in the bedroom.

I stood up, and he helped me take off my shirt, then he slid my leggings down my legs.

"Fuck," he breathed when he came face-to-face with my bare pussy. I definitely skipped panties today on purpose.

I stepped out of the leggings but couldn't move before he knelt between my legs and wrapped his lips around my clit. "TJ," I panted.

His tongue lapped at my center while he slid two thick fingers inside me. I rocked against him and almost came when he slammed a third finger inside.

"Be a good girl and take it," he ordered.

I had no complaints about that. He licked and sucked on me while his fingers pumped in and out until I was screaming his name and clutching at his hair.

"Good girl," he cooed as he looked up at me with that lopsided grin. He pulled back and wiped his mouth with the back of his hand. "Get on the bed on your hands and knees. I'm gonna take you from behind tonight."

I bit my lip to keep from whimpering.

"You like that, right, baby girl?" he asked. He was still giving me that naughty grin.

I nodded.

He gave me a little tap on my butt. "Good. Now get on the bed."

I did as he asked, climbing into the bed and getting up onto all fours. TJ took his time getting in behind me. His lips traveled up my spine and tickled me, but I tried to hold in my giggle. He was in a demanding mood tonight, but I liked that he needed to be aggressive and have his way with me tonight.

He opened the bedside drawer, and I heard him slip a condom on and spread lube across his cock. He reached down to spread the excess amount against my entrance.

"I love you," he whispered in my ear when he finally pressed inside me.

I groaned at the impact and gripped the sheets in front of me. "Love you too, baby."

He gripped my hair while he moved inside me, hitting so deep I felt the sensation all throughout my body. "You better."

I pressed myself back against his groin, and he slammed inside me repeatedly. "I do," I moaned.

One of his hands gripped my hip, while the other tightened his grip on my hair. I liked when he gripped onto me or held me down on the bed. I never thought I would like that. TJ made me feel safe enough to let go of my guilt over my desires. Also, rough make-up sex was the absolute best.

"Right there," I moaned into my pillow. I clutched at the headboard with both hands, trying to steady myself as he spun me out of control.

"Be a good girl, and I'll make you come again," he growled into my ear. He reached a hand around and slid it across my clit.

"Please, TJ," I begged.

"Please what?"

I could almost see his grin even though my eyes were closed and I had slumped against the bed onto my stomach.

"Ride me hard. Give it to me rough."

"Fuck yes," he growled, and he did as I asked, driving deep inside me while he held my hair in his fist. The tinge of pain on my scalp was a welcome sensation as I tumbled down into the depths of my orgasm.

"TJ," I moaned.

"Come for me."

"I am," I cried out and felt the wave of pleasure wash over me.

He rode me hard while I laid against the pillow in post-orgasm bliss. It wasn't long before he roared behind me and spurted his release into the condom.

He pressed a tiny kiss onto my shoulder before he pulled out. He got rid of the condom and slid back into the bed a moment later. He pulled me onto his chest, and I sighed in contentment while he ran his fingers through my hair and soothed my scalp. "I wasn't too rough?" he asked. He had gripped my hair a little tighter than normal, but I kind of liked it.

I shook my head. "Nope. You know I love doggy."

He grinned at me. "Yeah, you do, you dirty girl."

I moved to my side and smiled at him. "Your dirty girl."

"Damn right!" he cheered, but I saw him wince from the bruising on his lower abdomen.

I slid my hand down his torso and lightly grazed over the bruised skin. He flinched at my touch. "It hurts?"

He shrugged it off. "Nothing I can't handle."

I got out of bed and threw on his t-shirt. I ignored him asking where I was going while I went downstairs into the kitchen. I realized we never put away the lasagna, so I did that first and made sure the pan was soaking in the sink. I went into the freezer for an ice pack and wrapped it in a dishtowel.

Back upstairs in my room, TJ laid in my bed, scrolling through his phone. He smiled at me when I crawled into bed and placed the pack on his injury.

"Thanks, baby," he said with a dopey smile.

"I hate seeing you in pain. I know you can take it, but I hate seeing you wince like that."

His hazel eyes sparkled at me. "See? I love that you take care of me."

I gave him a grin. "Kei says you love that I baby you."

He laughed. "It's nice to be cared for and know someone will always be there for me when I need it."

I pressed a kiss on his forehead. "I'm glad you gave me a second chance."

"Of course I did. I told you, you're my girl. When you smile at me, you make my whole day brighter. Now get over here and give me cuddles."

I smiled at him. That was one thing that surprised me about TJ. He could be such a cuddle monster.

I let him wrap his arms around me, and I was careful not to jostle him. I knew his bruises weren't major, but I still wanted to care for him. He kissed the top of my head. "I love you, Maxine. And I'm done chasing you."

I grinned at him. "Well, good, because I'm tired of running. I love you, Tristan James Desjardins."

"Ha! Nobody ever asks what the 'J' stands for!"

"I asked Rox."

He grinned again and brought me down for another searing kiss.

I didn't know what the future held for us, but my heart was about to burst from happiness that he was by my side again. Things could only get better from here.

EPILOGUE

TWO YEARS LATER
TJ

"Are you sure about this?" my twin sister asked me for the third time.

I paced in the room Max and I were sharing this week at my parents' cottage. Hockey season was over, and our family was spending a week of relaxation and fun at the lake.

Except for me. I was having a tiny meltdown about what I planned on doing this week.

"Do you think she won't like the ring?" I asked.

I opened the box and looked down at the simple princess cut engagement ring. The square-shaped diamond wasn't too big, but it was elegant and pretty, just like Max, and not too showy. I wanted something that symbolized my love for her but also matched her down-to-earth style.

Rox shook her head. "Max will love it. It's classy yet simple. But are you ready for this commitment?"

"Roxie, I want the two-point-five kids and the white picket fence. Maybe even the big house in the suburbs, too."

She made a face at my dreams. My sister was staunchly against marriage and kids, but not me. I always wanted a wife and a family to come home to. I wanted so badly for Max to be my forever...but I was worried she'd say no. We've been together for about two years now, but I had just convinced her to move in with me.

Rox pursed her dark-colored lips and gave me a hard look. "I want to make sure you really want this, and it's not because Mom's been pressuring you."

"I'm ready. I want her to be my forever."

Rox nodded in understanding. "Okay, good answer. She might expect it, though. She thought it was weird I wanted to get our nails done together before we left for vacation."

"Thanks for persuading her," I said and shoved the ring box back into my pocket.

When I told my sister I wanted to propose to Max when we came up to the lake for a family vacation, she jumped at the chance to help me plan. But I still didn't have a fleshed-out plan, and I was contemplating chickening out.

"When are you gonna do it?" Rox asked.

I shrugged. "Not sure yet. When we're alone, probably. Maybe take her somewhere nice in town. Or out on the boat?" I ran a hand through my hair. Every time I thought about how to do it, I froze up. I wanted everything to be perfect for her.

Rox opened her mouth, but then the door of the bedroom slammed open, and Benny walked in. "Hey! There you are. Your mom was wondering where you two ran off to."

After a day of relaxing both in and out of the water, Mom and Dad were in the mad rush of getting dinner ready. Benny had been bonding with my dad at the grill while Max was helping my mom in the kitchen. With our partners preoccupied, I pulled Rox into my room to help calm my nerves.

Rox smiled up at him. "Hey, love. Sorry, Tristan needed my advice."

Benny's dark eyes widened in understanding. "Oh!"

I glared at my twin. "You told him?"

"Bro, she tells me everything. Don't ya, angel?"

Rox beamed at him and stood on her tiptoes to give him a small kiss. "Of course I do, love. Let's get out of Tristan's hair and give him time to think."

They glided out of the room, leaving me with my thoughts and the engagement ring burning a hole in my pocket. I had to do it this week, but it had to be perfect. I just didn't know what that meant. I sighed and tried not to let my nerves get the best of me.

I went into the kitchen but only found Mom. She gave me a knowing smile. "Where's Max?" I asked.

She gestured toward the porch outback. "She wasn't feeling well, so she went to get some air."

I furrowed my brow.

Right before we left for this vacation, Max complained about being too tired. Things were busy at work now that she got promoted to social media manager and she was hosting the team podcast for the wives and girlfriends. I thought she was burning herself out. She got sick in the rental car on the way to the cottage yesterday, but I thought that was just car sickness. Worry tightened across my chest. I hated it when my girl wasn't feeling well.

Mom walked over to the fridge and handed me a can of ginger ale. "Maybe too much sun today. Give this to her," she said, but she had a smile on her face like she knew something I didn't.

"Thanks," I muttered.

I walked outside and waved to my dad while he was in the middle of telling a heyday story to Benny. Rox was rolling her eyes because this story morphed every time Dad told it. Benny appeased him, though, because he would rather be in Dad's good graces in case he made Benny bag skate again.

I walked down to the dock and found Max sitting on it, with her feet in the water, but her back was to me. I sat next to her and startled her so much, she put her hand against her heart.

"Jiminy Cricket! You scared me!" she exclaimed.

I grinned at her cute way of not-swearing and handed her the can of ginger ale. "Mom said you're not feeling well."

She frowned but took a tiny sip of her drink. She nervously pushed her hair behind her ear, looking down at her feet in the water. Max's anxiety would never go away, but I recognized the signs when she was struggling with something. I wanted to take all that pain away from her, wrap her in my arms, and tell her everything would be okay.

"Baby girl, what's wrong?"

She shook her head.

"Hey, tell me."

When she turned toward me, her eyes brimmed with tears, and that made my chest ache. "Please, don't get mad at me."

I cupped her face. "Baby, whatever it is, you can tell me. I'm here for you, always."

"It wasn't car sickness. And I wasn't just stressed from work last week."

I raised an eyebrow. "Okay?"

She sighed and pulled something out of her pocket and handed it to me. My eyes widened when I realized what the stick in my hand was. Then I stared down at the small rectangular window where the words 'pregnant' read in clear text.

Holy fucking shit.

NO WAY!

I looked up at her for confirmation, and she nodded solemnly.

"Really?" I croaked out.

She nodded. "I'm so sorry, I know we didn't—"

She stopped talking when I set the test down and stood up. I grabbed her hand and brought her to her feet in a flash. Her eyes widened when I got down on one knee and held the ring box out to her. "Maxine Monroe, I love you with all my heart, and this is the best news you could have ever given me. I want you to be my forever. Will you marry me?"

Her mouth formed an 'O,' and she put her hands to her mouth. "TJ. You can't... It's not just because of the baby? You really want this?"

"Of course I do! I didn't even know about the baby until right this second. This isn't exactly how I planned to propose, but...I want to wake up every day with you beside me. I want to dry your tears and comfort you when your nightmares get too much. To be your rock when you need me. And I want you to baby me when I get injured because I love how you take care of me, even when I tell you I'm a tough guy who can take it. I want all of that with you by my side."

"SAY YES ALREADY!" Benny and Rox yelled from the porch.

We both laughed and turned around to see my parents,

Benny, and Rox all watching us intently from up on the porch. I was still on one knee, waiting for Max to give me her answer. This was definitely not the romantic gesture I had thought about, but finding out she was carrying our baby was the hockey gods way of telling me it was time. That if I didn't ask her right here and now, no other time would be perfect.

"Maxine Monroe," I began again.

"Gosh! Yes, of course I want to marry you, Tristan. I love you so much. I didn't want you to be mad about the baby."

She held out her neatly manicured hand to me, and I slid the ring onto her finger. It fit perfectly, like it had been made just for her. She looked like she was glowing as she smiled—but maybe that was the pregnancy.

Holy fuck, we were having a baby! I wanted to be a dad so badly. I didn't think it would happen so soon, but I was excited.

She stared down at her finger and admired the ring; then she narrowed her eyes at me as I stood up. "Is this why Rox begged me to get our nails done before we left?"

I gave her my famous lopsided grin. "Guilty. Do you like the ring?"

She beamed. "It's perfect. It's not too big or flashy, just a simple, elegant ring. I love it."

I slid a hand between us on her stomach. "I can't wait to make you my wife and get to meet our baby."

She cringed. "You're really not mad?"

I shook my head. "Nah, baby girl, we both had a part in this. I really want to be a dad. I wasn't expecting it to happen so soon, but I can't wait."

She smiled up at me. "How did I get so lucky with you?"

I pressed my forehead against hers. "I chased you."

She laughed. "I'm so glad you did. I love you so much, Tristan James Desjardins. I can't wait to marry you and watch you be the best daddy you can be."

I grinned at her and slanted my mouth against her lips, putting all the happy feelings I couldn't express into the kiss. My lady was carrying my child, and she was going to be my wife, and I couldn't imagine being happier.

I pulled away and grinned at her again. "You know twins run in the family, right?"

She groaned. "Shut your face! I think your mom already knows. She kept mentioning that she's a twin and that it runs in your family."

I remembered how Mom had grinned excitedly at me before I came outside to find Max. Mom totally knew.

"I love you, baby girl. You're mine forever and ever, and I can't wait to meet our baby."

"I'm yours," she agreed. "You won't ever have to chase me again."

Then she pulled me down for another passionate kiss while my family yelled obnoxiously in the background. But I paid them no mind as I kissed the love of my life and the mother of my unborn child. Maxine was mine, and I was hers. I never thought I'd be worthy of her love, but I was so glad I fought for the petite woman in my arms. I was never ever chasing her again.

ACKNOWLEDGMENTS

I know this book has been a long time coming, and a lot of you have been desperately waiting on TJ's book. I hope you all love it!

TJ and Maxine were probably my most challenging couple I've written. TJ's really not who you think he is, and you got to see in this one just how vulnerable, yet sweet, he can be. I think Dinah's 'lovable douche' comment from Take The Shot still rings true. Both of these two are hot messes, but I love them.

There are a lot of people I have to thank for helping me with this book. My betas—Becky, Chris, Jim, Kat, J Lynn, and Sophie. I appreciate your honest feedback for every book. Thanks so much for helping me with this one again.

Thanks to Kat Obie, J Lynn Autumn, and Sophie Masters for being a part of my critique group and helping me with this book. Also for letting me vent when I was really worried about it.

Big thanks to Charlie Knight again for editing the book! I am so happy you didn't hate this, because I had some worries. I can't wait to continue to work with you on the rest of the series.

The Bulldogs will return for another book sometime in 2023! So stay tuned for Blaise Holmstrom's book in The Fake Out. Yes, he's getting traded home to Philly! I can't wait to bring you my Philly-bred hockey player.

And lastly, thanks to all the readers who have taken a chance on me. I hope you continue to enjoy this series.

ALSO BY DANICA FLYNN

PHILADELPHIA BULLDOGS

Take The Shot

Score Her Heart

Against The Boards

MACGREGOR BROTHERS BREWING COMPANY

Accidentally In Love

Trapped In Love

Temporarily In Love

ABOUT THE AUTHOR

Danica Flynn is a marketer by day, and a writer by nights and weekends. AKA she doesn't sleep! She is a rabid hockey fan of both The Philadelphia Flyers and the Metropolitan Riveters. When not writing, she can be found hanging with her partner, playing video games, and reading a ton of books.

CPSIA information can be obtained
at www.ICGtesting.com
Printed in the USA
BVHW030847090622
639304BV00006B/79

9 781957 494012